eXtinction RATED

AN AUTOFICTIONAL DARK SATIRE ABOUT GOOD AND EVIL

ALAN CLEMENTS

WORLD DHARMA PUBLICATIONS

EXTINCTION X-RATED

AN AUTOFICTIONAL DARK SATIRE
ABOUT GOOD AND EVIL

World Dharma Publications
2768 West Broadway
Suite 74709
Vancouver, B.C., Canada V6K 2G4

Cover design by World Dharma Publications
Typography by World Dharma Publications

Library of Congress Cataloging-in-Publication Data
Clements, Alan 1951 —

EXTINCTION X-RATED:
AN AUTOFICTIONAL DARK SATIRE ABOUT GOOD AND EVIL
Alan Clements
p. cm.
ISBN: 978-1-953508-20-1 (alk. paper)

1. Liberty — freedom — Buddhism 2. Spiritual life — Buddhism
— non-sectarian— mindfulness 3. Human rights — all aspects 4. Social,
Political and Environmental justice — all 5. Activism — all 6.
Consciousness — all 7. Politics — global 8. Body, Mind & Spirit
9. Satire, comedy, dark comedy, gallows humor – all

BQ7657. F7 C87 2009 292. 3 777
— March 1, 2021
First printing, March 15, 2021
ISBN: 978-1-953508-20-1
Printed in USA on acid-free, recycled paper
10 9 8 7 6 5 4 3 2

ABOUT ALAN CLEMENTS

Alan Clements is a satirist, performing artist, former Buddhist monk, and investigative journalist in areas of war and extreme conflict. He is also the author of numerous books, a spoken word album, and the subject of a feature documentary film. His work has been endorsed by President Jimmy Carter, numerous Nobel Laureates, celebrities, and thought leaders worldwide. Alan has been interviewed by the New York Times, Time and Newsweek Magazines, CNN, BBC, Voice of America, ABC, CBS, and Democracy Now, along with Utne Reader, *Yoga* Journal, and Mother Jones. He has presented to such organizations as Mikhail Gorbachev's State of The World Forum, The Soros Foundation, United Nations Association of San Francisco, the universities of California, Toronto, Sydney, and many others, including a keynote address at the John Ford Theater for Amnesty International's 30th year anniversary. For more information, AlanClements. com or WorldDharma.com

ALSO BY ALAN CLEMENTS

A Future to Believe In: 108 Reflections on the Art and Activism
of Freedom

Instinct for Freedom: Finding Liberation Through Living

Wisdom for the World: Alan Clements in Conversation
with Sayadaw U Pandita

The Voice of Hope: Alan Clements in Conversation with
Aung San Suu Kyi
Edition I: 1997 & Edition II: 2007

Burma: The Next Killing Fields?

Natural Freedom: The Dharma Beyond Buddhism
Produced by Sounds True and World Dharma Productions

Spiritually Incorrect: An Existential Anti-War Comedy
Produced and edited by Ian Mackenzie

Burma's Revolution of the Spirit (Photographic Tribute)
By Alan Clements and Leslie Kean

Beyond Rangoon – A Feature Film Directed by John Boorman
Script Revisionist and Principle Consultant

Burma's Voices of Freedom: Conversations with Alan Clements
An Ongoing Struggle for Democracy (Four Volume Set)
By Alan Clements and Fergus Harlow

Spiritually Incorrect: The Life and Rebel Wisdom of Alan Clements
Film Directed by Peter Downy & Produced by United Natures Media

Freedom: Acts of Conscience – A Double Album on Spotify
Produced by World Dharma Productions & Jeffrey Hellman
with Music by In Text

"Your Silence Will Not Protect You."

— AUDRE LORDE

PROLOGUE

This book was never intended to be published. Rather, it was written as a form of existential self-therapy, to discover new inner landscapes and abide more honestly and courageously in conscience and dignity.

Essentially, I wanted to ask myself the most pressing questions I'd been living with: In the face of the sixth mass extinction, is there hope and is it realistic? What do you fear and why? How are you in denial? Where are you folded? And how do you lie to yourself? And if so, what is it that you are hiding or afraid of?

On a practical note, this work, for purely literary reasons, is auto-fiction – a novel situated somewhere between fiction and non-fiction, with a first-person narrative. As such, there is absolutely no attempt to depict people, places, and events accurately, my own and or others.

With that said, everything in the book occurred at some point in my life, whether as an outer real world experience or a fantasy made real on my own dreamscape. In that sense, this book is the deliberate creation of a conceptual mandala – an intersecting set of free flowing symbols and realities, both provocative and playful, designed to awaken my own latent potentials and liberate limiting identities.

On a cautionary note, stand forewarned: if offended by expletives or graphic images of sexuality and violence, please do yourself a favor and close this book, as in read no further. I spared nothing in discovering my own uncensored edge and the challenging process of coming to terms with that raw new reality.

In addition, the book is neither a disguised eulogy nor a prayer to confront the madness, although both are partially true. Equally, it's a self-guided meditation designed as existential entertainment – a cathartic collage of satirical stories laced with (at times) dark humor.

As an expression of creative activism, the book confronts established notions of power, both political and spiritual. It asks us to face the incomprehensible. To look into the abyss itself and breathe together. Bearing witness through imagination, invoking humor, maybe not laughter, in response to the horrors of the everyday world.

As a purely creative act, I wanted to break free of artifice and taboos and cross boundaries – venturing into the unnerving frontiers of spontaneous authenticity. By challenging all forms of self-censorship, I created an experience that you may love, or you may hate or may be confounded by.

In the end the book is a prayer, a protest and a scream. As it challenges propaganda and totalitarianism, while (I pray) serving to safeguard freedom of thought, conscience, and expression. To me, freedom, dignity, and the universality of human rights are the vanguard of sanity and the best protection against racism, violence, and war.

I do hope you are mindful throughout the read, in

that you allow for a range of emotions to arise and see where they may lead. With that said, thank you for going along on this journey with me.

Alan Clements

Los Angeles March 21, 2021

THE HOUSE OF ROCKY

I'm sitting alone in the house of my dear friend Robert Chartoff – the Oscar winning producer of thirty-nine feature films, including The Right Stuff, Raging Bull, New York New York, They Shoot Horses Don't They, The Gambler, Valentino, and Rocky – the most influential boxing film of all time, featuring Sylvester Stallone as Rocky Balboa.

"Winning the Academy Award for Best Picture was a total surprise," Bob once told me. "The New York Times had given it one of the most scathing reviews, ever. But that very night, at the premier, to our astonishment, Rocky, our "sentimental slum movie," got a standing ovation.

"As the film swept the nation," Bob went onto explain, "audiences stood up everywhere – aroused by Rocky's spirit of invincibility and FIGHT.

"Rocky created a new American archetype," Bob continued. "That of believing in yourself, with zero-self-doubt – a tireless courage with NO obstacle, physical or psychological, too great to overcome.

"Most of all," Bob would encourage me. "FIGHT for YOUR DREAM, Alan, and NEVER GIVE UP."

That was the Bob I came to know, and so much more. Yet, as I sit in his House of Rocky in the isolation of mandatory lockdown, with millions of Covid deaths worldwide, I'm devoid of both fight and hope. Ironically, I felt a similar pain at about the same time as Rocky's release, when I left this very city of Los Angeles with the intention of ordaining as a Buddhist monk in Burma, to enter my own ring and the fight of my life.

At the time, there were no other options, so it seemed. Either suffocate in LA, caged in a claustrophobic capitalistic culture as an opiate-dependent artist trying to process my struggle through alcohol, *yoga*, and painting, or risk entering a remote totalitarian country ruled by a ruthless military dictator and meditate in a monastery for the rest of my life.

And here it is nearly fifty years later, after thousands of hours of meditation, mindfulness and MDMA-assisted psychotherapy, and the world has only gotten worse, and my life too.

As a result of this truth, the options I set forth for myself today are clear: either find a reason to live or end my life before midnight.

Suicide, or mindful euthanasia, as I preferred to call it, has been on my mind for some years now. Beyond the pandemic, mass paranoia and the porno politics of America's psychosis, it's been a tough time.

Among the challenges, multiple deaths: both parents, only months apart; my beloved meditation teacher of forty years; my godmother, whom I adored; my two remaining aunts, and three best men friends – gone, all unexpectedly.

There were other challenges, as well. A betrayal and

the collapse of a relationship just months before marriage; a thinly veiled death threat; a murder in the family, followed by a suicide with a bullet to the head; a tortuous legal battle for access to my daughter; the loss of a lucrative book and film deal, canceled, based on lies and distortions; a devastating case of the virus and with it the loss of smell and taste, along with ongoing chest and joint pains; a debilitating case of spinal osteoporosis requiring neck and back braces, and the sleepless nights, every night, unless I take the meds.

In truth, I could manage these annoyances, more or less. But the deeper despair was existential and far greater. That of societal collapse and near-term extinction – the absolute end of life, as we know it.

To amplify matters, the DOOMSDAY CLOCK was moved up to 100 seconds before midnight.

What is the DOOMSDAY CLOCK?

On their website we read: "Founded in 1945 by University of Chicago scientists who had helped develop the first atomic weapons in the Manhattan Project, the Bulletin of the Atomic Scientists created the Doomsday Clock two years later, using the imagery of apocalypse (midnight) and the contemporary idiom of nuclear explosion (countdown to zero) to convey threats to humanity and the planet. The decision to move (or to leave in place) the minute hand of the Doomsday Clock is made every year by the Bulletin's Science and Security Board in consultation with its Board of Sponsors, which includes eight Nobel laureates. The Clock has become a universally recognized indicator of the world's vulnerability to catastrophe from nuclear weapons, climate change, and disruptive technologies in other domains."

Could it be true that 300,000 years of human LIFE and millions of non-human species too are in our final few seconds?

Frankly, from my own research, 100 seconds felt generous. Not only from an out of control contagion, or an economic depression the likes of which the world has never seen. Or Trump's revenge from a "fraudulent election." Or the psychological toll of long-term lockdowns or the fall out of mandatory vaccinations. Or the incessant sirens from break-ins, assaults, and robberies. Or the tsunami of communist-infused totalitarianism engulfing the world. Or the Great Reset and the corporate capitalist coup well underway. But, the elephant in the room was how many informed people are saying that the climate collapse is irreversible, the Green New Deal is propaganda, mass starvation is near, and moreover, there's absolutely NO WAY of stopping our fetishism for consumerism, the death of nature, and human extinction.

David Suzuki, the preeminent environmental scientist and climate expert, was even more blunt in his bleak prognosis of the future of humanity, saying: "Us earthlings are in a giant car heading towards the brick wall of self-annihilation and everyone's arguing over where they're going to sit."

Why bicker over spiritual platitudes, political mumbo-jumbo and conspiratorial rabbit holes, when the sixth mass extinction is occurring at a pace far faster than the five previous extinctions combined, including the Great Dying some 252 million years ago that wiped out 90% of all Life?

The existential wall of extinction terrified me, but it was envisioning the final dystopian seconds before midnight that compelled me to consider my own painless release through mindful euthanasia.

I took out the 500 micrograms of acid I brought for this special occasion – a final fight to possibly lift me higher and give me a sense of hope to carry on – while on the other hand, I took out a perfectly lethal amount of morphine in a clear plastic syringe to take my life, should that be the more enlightened action, before the stroke of midnight.

I held both futures in the same hand and contemplated which one first and which one last? As I reflected on the two options, I heard the Doomsday Clock ticking in my head, which reminded me how long I had been planning this sacred moment. And now that it was here, there was a strange sense of excitement to be so close to a final truth.

CALLING FOR CLARITY

After an hour-long meditation of listening to my heart, I cranked "Eye of the Tiger" – the theme song of Rocky – and rose to the occasion. Left the syringe of morphine on its side, drank down the acid with organic Red Bull, and strutted around the room as if readying to enter the ring with the Devil himself. And as I danced, I heard Bob in my mind saying, "Alan, the bell has rung. The fight has begun."

But my surge of vitality was short lived, as I doubted myself. "Is hope a fantasy?" I asked. "Is the climate collapse truly irreversible? Are we really past the tipping point? As in over the cliff? Is extinction baked in? As in, no way to stop from hitting the wall? Or even slowing the Clock down? And if we could, how?"

I sat down in Bob's favorite chair and reflected on my dear friend, looking for direct access to his spirit and inspiration.

Bob was both an elegant pragmatist and a hardcore fighter. He came from poverty in the Bronx, went onto Union College and Columbia University Law School, and then drove to Hollywood at thirty, knowing no one and nothing about the film industry.

Here he hustled, making connections, learning the business, and moreover, never giving up. As a lawyer with charm and integrity, he quickly won the hearts of fledgling stars and studio heads who made deals.

Through an unflinching drive, a golden thumb, and an innovative sense of storytelling, Bob quickly reached producer stardom and the heights of Hollywood celebrity. Known for his lavish parties, and astute professionalism, he drew some of the most gifted talent into his productions, including Martin Scorsese, Robert De Niro, John Boorman, Lou Carlino, Ken Russell, Sam Jackson, Philip Kaufman, Julie Taymor, Tom Wolfe, Rudolf Nureyev, Sam Shepard, Lee Marvin, Sylvester Stallone and many dozens of other greats.

Bob once told me, with a wry laugh, how he was offered the role of producing the Beatles before they came to America, but turned it down "to remain focused on film-making and myth-making."

Bob was in every sense an icon of the AMERICAN DREAM. Whereas ROCKY was the crown jewel of his own archetypal expression of rags to riches, and an offering to everyone who was ever at their bottom, that they too can fight back to achieve their dream.

Bob was a brilliant friend and today I'm reminded of his fighting spirit, when he called from the hospital and said, "Alan, the doctor just left and told me they found 'an inoperable cancerous tumor on my pancreas and I have three weeks to live.'"

After a long silence, he concluded, "I'm calling to say I love you. Our friendship speaks for itself. It has brought me some of the most memorable moments of my life."

We talked for a while longer, until he concluded, with a halting voice, while holding back tears: "Remember, Alan, and I've told you many times. You're among the finest talent I've ever known. Use your gifts – your voice, your heart, your storytelling, your genius. And NEVER GIVE UP."

Bob did not go easily. He fought on and, defying medical certainty, lived for another two years. In part, not only because of his tireless spirit of Rocky, but his deep and genuine spiritual grace. Along with the epic support of his beloved wife, Jenny, who devoted herself with saintly service to the man of her dreams, right up to his final breath here in this very House of Rocky on June 10, 2015.

I was blessed to have married them back in 1990, after a long courtship.

CONTEMPLATING THE END

As the acid came on, I dove deep inside searching for evidence of hope to face yet another day, while honoring this sacred space as a gift from Jenny, as she retreated to their country farm in Canada to be near family and shelter with their daughter from the Covid storm.

As a temporary oasis, with no future known, I reflected, there's no monastery to escape to; no home to go; no parents to see; no partner to embrace; no trauma to heal; no book to read to guide me home; no retreat to conduct; nothing to do other than to CRY and FEEL. And look more honestly into the abyss.

Here we are, 8 billion of us on this tiny orb; a self-annihilating selfie-obsessed species careening over the cliff. And with us, taking out millions of non-human species into the sixth mass extinction. Yet, we do little to nothing to change our ways, and blindly follow in the footsteps of Einstein's infamous dictum: "Insanity is doing the same thing over and over and expecting different results."

Are WE merely a two-legged flesh-draped species of magical thinking zombies programmed by a malevolent DNA to kill, rape and self-destruct, and repeat it epoch by epoch with a smile of denial? Why are we fighting over politics and ownership and race and color and creed, rather than nurturing a love of nature and finding bridges of co-operation, sustainability and peaceful co-existence? Or do we all deserve to crash and burn and die, and rid our Mother Earth of this genocidal deviant strain called human life?

I see a large hardback book on the table in front of me: It's the "Complete Collection of Cartoons from the New Yorker Magazine." I thumb through it slowly as if excavating the ancient ruins of Western civilization for dark comedic clues of how to save the world from the plague of human hubris.

I turn to a page that stops me: there's a man mindfully poised – as if frozen in his stillness at a fork in the road. I entered the cartoon and let it speak to me. The left fork had a sign that read: "the life you could have led." And the right fork read: "the life you will lead."

And I'm thinking, isn't that the essential dilemma of the human experience: life is the result of choices; good ones and bad ones; a never-ending set of crossroads – weekly, hourly, every second – every movement – choices; wise ones, dumb ones and numb ones.

With every inhalation of a cigarette, is now the time to stop? Every drink, give me just one more and I'll quit. Every page of a book turned; every word read. Every letter chosen in a text. Every breath. Every divorce and every hour of legal fees started with a kiss at the crossroads. If only I wasn't color blind and hadn't translated the red flag for green. So much for chemistry as a guide to wise choices.

Oh, for God's sake, Alan, I retorted. You of all people know there is only NOW and all roads lead back to the PRESENT – which, brought my mindfulness back to the morphine in front of me and I imagined how easy it would be to inject.

But instead of ending the future, I closed my eyes in mindful reflection on the past – a free flowing serendipity of how I arrived at this final crossroads of either ongoing life, or a mindful death.

BE HERE NOW

Here on the 50th anniversary of my spiritual career that began with reading former-Harvard professor Richard

Alpert's infamous magical thinking classic, "BE HERE NOW," on ACID, no less. Two habits I still can't break, even today.

The book, by Baba Houdini Dass, is a masterpiece in self-deception and served in the day as a psychedelicized western BIBLE of re-appropriated Hindu propaganda. That, from a discerning Dawkin-esque point of view, reads more like a modern-day Manchurian Candidate – the cult classic in brainwashing – than a manual in mindful spiritual transformation, as it was meant to be.

To be fair, I counted well over 100 religious fantasies in it today before deciding to drop the acid. And stopped only because I began to feel nauseous, as in, how could I have been so naive, believing, at the time, that wonky ACID drenched, platitudinal, pseudo-spiritual crap?

Spiritually Intelligent me, albeit only 19 back then, within hours of ingesting that mesmerizing sacred-drivel and having my freewill high-jacked, I felt like I was lifted from a low hanging depression and rejuvenated on cognitive God crack.

All I wanted to do was to hitchhike overland to India, don a loin cloth, and live as an acid-dropping mendicant chanting Om on the banks of the Ganges, doing *yoga* on temple grounds and, if successful, fondling the white succulent breasts and vegetarian *yoni*s of my Hindu-hypnotized female Western students, and count my donations at night.

Not so lucky. I played it safe and stayed Stateside, diving into the more accessible ideological prison camp of the NOW. That hallowed wonderland that all Saints figured out as the ONLY TRUE PORTAL into ELIGHTENMENT and UNCONDITIONAL BLISS. Meanwhile, judging the shit out of everyone who was not on the same sacred path as me.

Tragically, living in the 'now' turned out to be one of the biggest mind heists in modern history; the Wall Street for the spiritual set. Once present, you add 'deep listening' and soon you're accessing your 'heart's wisdom' to guide you along life's moment to moment crossroads. And with it, down the digital rabbit hole into my next online teacher training on the sacred art of embodied denial.

Simultaneous to my discovery of 'the moment,' and with it my rapidly maturing spiritual career, I continued my aberrant pursuit of MONEY.

Forced from age 11 to work at my Dad's Esso station pumping gas, I learned that money mattered. And since I was not yet ready to transcend the world and wander India as a renunciate, the NOW, as I wanted to reclaim it, was a lot more fulfilling with cash in my account rather than always almost empty.

So, entrepreneurial me opened a string of successful non-alcoholic night clubs on the East Coast. I was 20 at the time and wanted to provide a safe haven within the American war culture for young adults – to meet up in a smoke-and alcohol-free environment, and hang with great music, plenty of sofas, fruit drinks, and dozens of Foosball tables, and the country's first video games.

Within days, local TV picked up on our groundbreaking alt-life genius and did stories on us highlighting our packed smoke-free clubs. Although parents loved the vision, it didn't go over well with the local authorities.

After being raided by a dozen baton bashing angry Atlanta policemen, I along with fifty or so kids were jailed. I was charged with running a disorderly house, a sex den, and drug trafficking. "Why else would so many kids be there," the police chief shouted at me, "if you weren't selling dope, sex and cigarettes under the table?"

As we walked into the courtroom for my jury-less trail my attorney stated matter-of-factly, "the only way to avoid a multi-year prison term, that I might add, includes rape by other inmates," was to close my clubs, pay a 25k cash fine and agree to a two-year ban from reentering the state of Georgia.

Paid the fine, did a fire sale of my clubs to the local Mafia that the lawyer arranged, and doubled down on my spiritual life by moving with my partner to Hawaii – the emerging Mecca of East meets West in America.

SAMSARA

My partner and I were free-thinking vegetarian outlaws, somewhere between artists, entrepreneurs, hippies, and renegades. And so our rebellious manner blended right in with the other high-end spiritualized drop outs, mostly from Beverly Hills, Malibu, and the Palisades, living on the white sand beaches of Kauai. All of us naked, doing *yoga*, dropping acid, eating mangoes and mushrooms, smoking pot, and endlessly walking and talking about the *dharma*, while continuing to practice LIFE ONLY in the NOW.

Who could have imagined at the time just how big a business HUMAN TRANSFORMATION would become, with high end trainings in mindfulness, *yoga*, meditation, psychedelics, coaching, cuddling, cumming, and cultural reappropriation? And with it, the festishizing of purity and self-improvement.

And now, I asked myself, teetering on the edge of awakened suicide, am I mired in self-deception and if so, how am I perpetuating extinction, other than in every way a nature-blind-consumer does?

But we're all in this together, I reminded myself as I read Martin Luther King's eloquent decree: "We're all caught in an inescapable network of mutuality, tied in a single garment of destiny. Whatever affects one directly, affects all indirectly."

At one point in my life his words inspired creative activism, but today through the truth-illuminating lens of LSD and mindful self-honesty, I contracted. Forced as it were, to be a prisoner of my unconsciousness and others too, while slaving within this "inescapable network" of insanity, along with its billions of weavers co-creating a suffocating quilt of extinction.

And what is this "network of mutuality" we are doomed to share at this time?

A panic-driven pandemic with violence through the roof; alcohol, opioids and other pharmaceuticals at all-time highs; evictions and bankruptcies by the millions; the death of small business; anarchy in the Capital and on city streets; people buying guns and pit bulls; a spike in suicides; hate crimes intensifying by the day; a pedophilia-protecting Pope in the pocket of the Communist Party of China; and with no shortage of deranged Prime Ministers and Presidents and profiteering politicians furthering plans for a totalitarian world.

It all feels like too much; far darker than the Spanish Flu and the great depression, and those 250 million deaths by war that followed.

What's new, I reminded myself.

The Buddha, 26 centuries before, called it *SAMSARA*: an infinite center-less house of mental and physical conditions with intersecting inner and outer environments, burning, as they were, with the fire of hatred, greed, and war. And we earthlings, trapped in a photonic bubble, orbiting an inferno – and soon to be engulfed by her flames. The very star that keeps us warm, grows our food and keeps us suntanned, will soon grill us like baked bass.

Meanwhile, the anesthesia of greed keeps us fixated with our toys – cars, phones, refineries, casinos, nukes, stocks, politics, vitriol, and conspiracy theories. On and on SAMSARA swirls, as if Earth were a circus wheel of eternal consumerism with purchasable thrills and screams.

Meanwhile, we learn to meditate to chill the inner heat and or to block it out altogether. And there are some who remain oblivious, and still others who translate the doom as a heavenly messenger to wake us up to the reality that our earthly home is ablaze with denial and greed, and with no way out. Or is there?

THE TRUTH OF S.H.I.T.

I thank Ram Dass for turning me onto the Buddha's First Noble Truth: The TRUTH of S.H.I.T. IS: S – for suffering. H – for horror. I – for idiocy. And T – for trauma. S.H.I.T. IS – a fact of life. The *Buddha* was said to have said, S.H.I.T. is the defining nature of *Samsara*.

No one would contest that it's shitty to be one of the 300,000 children starving in Yemen right now. Or how shitty it is to be a Buddhist nun immolating herself in Tibet in a non-media covered protest of her sister nuns being gang-raped in Chinese-run prisons by soldiers loyal to their Master, China's Premier Xi Jinping.

Imagine how shitty it is for the millions of Chinese slave laborers working 90-hour weeks assembling parts for the phone I use. And how shitty it is to be among the millions of unemployed without knowing where their next meal is coming from, while fat cat disassociated politicians wine and dine each other suffering over stimulus bills that support the rich. There are just so many ways to see the Truth of S.H.I.T.

In rare moments of self-honesty, I see the S.H.I.T. of my own hypocrisies. Trite little ones, like anticipating likes and swipes and views and comments and followers. Or bigger ones, like judgments and jealousies. The lure of beauty, status and wealth. The avoidance of loss and blame and the hunger for pleasure and fame. As if botoxing the wrinkles of time stopped the aging process of living.

The *Buddha's* Truth of S.H.I.T. is: Aging, he said, is shit. Disease is shit. Being associated with assholes is shit. Being separated from loved ones is shit. Mortality is shit. Being oppressed, shamed and shit on is shit. Not being able to control your mind is shit. And being censored and deplatformed and having your rights and freedoms taken from you is really shitty. There are so many expressions of S.H.I.T., the *Buddha* was said to have declared S.H.I.T as UNIVERSAL.

And central to S.H.I.T. is self-deception.

I had someone tell me how they regretted not getting in early on Facebook's stock. "I could have retired on Maui years ago," they said. "But foolish me, used the 10k on a mindfulness teacher training in LA."

I explained that personal data is the "new oil" industry and it's killing the planet. Facebook alone operates with at least 20 buildings, each one a square mile wide and five stories high. Each stacked with hundreds of thousands of fossil fuel-sucking mega-servers churning out tons of lethal gases to keep our friendships active, our selfies posted, and the maniacal censoring of speech deemed unconstitutional. And, if I am not mistaken, the majority of their 52,000 employees, along with their executive branch, are proud practitioners of mindfulness.

He could not see the connection. I agreed and conceded that I too use Facebook and I am also a consumer. And added, "I'm therefore a mindful hypocrite." To which he replied, "I'm not, I can't stand Zuckerberg and deleted my account and only use Instagram, Gab, and Google."

I comforted myself by reflecting that S.H.I.T. didn't originate with us. We are merely inheritors of the S.H.I.T. gene.

THE INDIAN REMOVAL ACT

Back in 1857, our prescient forefathers created the Indian Removal Act. As history holds it, our nation's thought leaders gathered in Washington D.C. to collectively cleanse the anguish of their own tortured childhoods and rid themselves of the historical trauma of centuries of mass murder by their white supremacist forefathers and mothers.

These courageous visionaries pushed beyond their ego barriers and committed themselves for the next 100 years of American spiritual development to ethnically cleanse our beloved NEW REPUBLIC of 15 million indigenous people. Who, mind you, were so depraved as to empower community, follow the laws of nature, meditate, smoke weed, and not kill each other over sex, race, stock options, oil, voter fraud, and slavery.

As the wisdom of the white man spread, so did his ancestral art of genocidal imperialism. And as the sacred purge swept our great nation, local populations that were spared rape and beheading courageously healed from their primordial toxic belief in peaceful co-existence.

As a result, future generations were largely spared, as the "genocide gene" slowly receded from the collective consciousness of our Elders. Until the healing was complete, at such time when our great leaders expanded their vision and waged "forever wars" to liberate the entire world from S.H.I.T.

And there were even special benefits awarded to those who so courageously desecrated life and inflicted the most enduring generational traumas on peace-loving peoples. These noble men went onto to become our Founding Parents – Presidents, Senators, Supreme Court Justices, and the wealthiest of landowners, bankers and insurance companies, and other corporate elites, manufacturing such peace and prosperity establishing visions as nuclear bombs, multiple rocket precision drones, digital firewalls, mass surveillance systems, an array of pharmaceutical drugs that would inspire depression, anxiety, dementia and even suicide, and chemicals so knowingly toxic they will kill the oceans and render agricultural lands impotent for centuries. Such were their legacies of greatness.

Mind you, this was long before the Swedish armaments and military weapon's manufacturer Alfred Nobel created the prestigious Norwegian Noble Peace Prize, coveted by visionaries of peace and nonviolence the world over. And significantly more prestigious than any title or position in government, religion, or big business.

Among the Nobel Committee's uncompromising commitment to award the prize ONLY to people of peace, they expanded its meaning to include such notable proponents of 'nonviolent war' and 'mass peaceful denigration' as Mikhail Gorbachev, Yitzhak Rabin, Yasser Arafat, and Henry Kissinger.

They even expanded the prize to include those dedicated to global consumerism, the nuclear arms race, climate collapse, the death of nature and human extinction itself, such as Al Gore, Barack Obama, and the European Union to name just a few.

And further, due to the Committee's unimpeachable moral standard, they did not award the prize to such impostors of peace and nonviolence as Mahatma

Gandhi, Eleanor Roosevelt, Burma's U Thant, Václav Havel, and Ken Saro-Wiwa, who the Committee applauded, by the way, as being appropriately hung for his challenge to Big Oil.

As the acid brought me back to my breath, Mark Twain's witticism seemed more apt than ever, when he said, "Don't part with your illusions. When they are gone, you may still exist, but you have ceased to live."

Indeed, I said. Fuck extinction. It will happen without us.

NAROPA 1974

By this point in my spiritual career, my partner and I were among the privileged few that flocked in the summer of '74 to Naropa Institute in Boulder, Colorado. Some called it a spiritual Woodstock, but it was more like a counter-culture flea market for 2,500 hippies and spiritual wannabes, punctuated with early-stage hustlers, bona fide hypocrites, and fully armored predators.

There was also a smorgasbord of ambitious self-appointed teachers, nerdy types who had never done acid nor danced to Zeppelin or the Cream, or even had sex other than with Thai prostitutes in Bangkok or Hindu hookers in Calcutta.

Some had just come back from the East touting their re-appropriated Asian personas and platitudes with phantasmagorical stories of super-lies of pseudo-saints with psychic powers and other enlightened tales laced with the hunger for legitimacy. Others hustled *dharma* 101, after becoming enlightened while smoking their first joint, or on day eight of yet another Goenka course.

A lot of us, on the other hand, after becoming hardened by the Kent State murders and campus activism to the war, were eager to know the ancient no-bullshit secrets of the East. Personally, I desperately wanted salvation from a sick American capitalist culture, with far too many come downs from acid, and no fucking desire to pursue a bullshit Ph.D.

I was curious with the scene but not smitten.

I had originally gone to Boulder from West Palm Beach where I was painting and exploring acid and *yoga*, after reading a small book on mindfulness meditation by Burma's Mahasi Sayadaw, on acid, again. It simply blew my mind, even more than "Be Here Now" did.

I remember standing in the bookstore reading, "Ignorance conceals the true nature of things and mindfulness reveals it. And progressively from the insight gained, liberation from greed, fear, and ignorance is achieved. Thus, the most important thing one can do in their lifetime is to practice intensive insight meditation." I was convinced on the spot.

Serendipitously, days later, when I saw a poster in a laundry-mat with Ram Dass' name as a headliner for this place called "Naropa Institute," along with an impossible to pronounce Tibetan Buddhist name, I said, sounds like this may be a go. When I read that Alan Ginsberg and John Cage would also be there, I said, done.

Ultimately, my heart was set on meeting someone who had been to Burma and could tell me about their meditative experiences with Mahasi Sayadaw.

As it turned out, in looking back at the Naropa crossroads, it was anything but a hip spiritual offering. Rather, it was a three month grooming session for some of the most manipulative sexual and financial predators in the "*dharma* scene."

It started with the very founder of Naropa, Chögyam Trungpa Rinpoche – Buddhism's very own Archbishop George Pell, the notorious righthand predator of Pope Francis, the man who was convicted of 37 years of systematic orifice stuffing of young children's faces, middles and rears with his Papal-endorsed penis.

Although Trungpa was hipper than Pell, or even all the other 10,000 or so priests combined accused of sexually violating underage children, he confined his predation to non-children students.

On the other hand, he was more violent than Pell and had the added attraction of being an incessantly drunk narcissistic reincarnation of a yet another former Tibetan priest. Perhaps he was even a Pope in a previous life.

As Ram Dass was a nonviolent deity worshiping God junkie, who brokered pseudo-psycho-therapeutic re-appropriated Hinduism, Trungpa was decidedly among the top three influential shyster-criminals to spread rebranded Buddhism in the West, something he called "crazy wisdom." Also known as, 'put your mouth around my thick dick and suck the wisdom from it,' with a little pat on the head after I cum.

Surprisingly, he attracted some of the West's most elite artists, writers, poets, and intellectuals at the time who willfully became complicit members of his crazy wisdom cult.

Among his contributions of bringing Buddhism to the West are the luminous *Shambhala* teachings, noted for liberating repressed fantasies of sexual predation, the art of enlightened alcoholism, and compassionate physical assault. All of which included many hundreds of his inner-most students, and even his beloved wife.

It was no surprise that many of his most gifted followers carried on the tradition after his farewell at age 47 from decades of alcohol abuse, a $40,000 dollar a year cocaine and barbiturate addiction, and a two-pack a day smoking habit. He did meditate, however, and was one of the early inspirations for the beginning of a Buddhist oriented AA recovery program in America.

Just before his untimely death, his genius compelled him to pass his perversities onto Ösel Tendzin – a Western student and his chosen *dharma* heir – who brilliantly expanded the crazy wisdom teachings by, after testing

HIV-positive, knowingly involved himself sexually with a number of close students, promising them no harm due to his holiness and *karmic* purity.

Several of them were blessed to die of crazy wisdom AIDS. And as legend has it, they were reborn in Tibet, and recognized as reincarnated High Priests. Apparently, some of them are continuing the crazy wisdom tradition behind enemy lines as Chinese soldiers dedicated to gang raping Tibetan Nuns, imprisoned for worshiping his Holiness the Dalai Lama, thereby ethnically cleansing them to be worthy followers of Premier Xi Jinping– the all compassionate Dictator of the Chinese Communist Party.

Sadly, the *Shambhala* Brand lives on today with Trungpa's very *on* son, Sir Siphon, and twenty years and counting of his own enlightened predation. And there are additional famous reincarnated bestselling rapist Rinpoches as well. Long live Tibetan Buddhism. Long live the Pope.

Yet another fine example of uncharted trauma being translated as spontaneous enlightenment.

And now, two hours into my own uncensored life and death crossroads, I wondered, after this early level of unexpected purging, if I had taken Ayahuasca instead of acid. I then quickly jumped naked into the pool to psychically cleanse myself and returned to the House of Rocky with renewed purpose and trust in the efficacy of the process to be symbolic of me, and no one else.

UNIVERSITY OF VIRGINIA

Just a few years before, in 1970, I was a coat and tie hippie freshman attending the prestigious University of Virginia, enjoying a full athletic scholarship to pursue any degree desired.

I was finally able to escape my long summer shifts working at my Dad's gas station in Norfolk Virginia – the epicenter of America's war machine and the largest military complex in the world. By entering UVA I felt that I had finally arrived in life. I was somebody. And moreover, I could become anyone at this point. The power was fully in my own hands.

UVA, the top party school in America according to Playboy, is the brainchild of the noblest of Americans, Tomas Jefferson – the third US President and founding father of our beloved Declaration of Independence.

Mr. Jefferson was so inspiring, there were times I wanted to follow in my adopted father's footsteps and give the presidency a run. With my renegade history in art, music, and LSD, I knew I had a long way to go to grow into a life in the White House, but anything felt possible at UVA.

In fact, a year earlier I had been elected senior class president of my high school, only to have the role taken from me a few days later, with the principal announcing to the student body the "election was fraudulent and the presidency goes to the real president." Regardless, I was undeterred and doubled down on my art and public speaking and experiments in consciousness with LSD, and of course, athletics.

And at UVA, who cared that Mr. Jefferson was a white supremacist and tortuously subjugated his hundreds of Black slaves. Who can blame him, really? Slavery and torture were baked into the American way of life long before he came along. He was just playing out his conditioning.

Nor did he have access to the transformational tools we have today. There was no cognitive therapy, no plant medicine, no Wisdom 2.0 Conferences to attend to learn mindful stress reduction, nothing.

I try to imagine the anxiety levels of him living in the cognitive dissonance, on the one hand, of being a Founding Father of our Great country's "All Men are Created Equal Brand" and on the other hand, being a poser and a white supremacist slave owner. And to think of his poor wife Martha, after learning that he had a child with her half-sister – his favorite sex slave – and the stress of burying his hypocrisy.

On the other hand, Richard Nixon was in the White House and had nowhere near the courage of Jefferson to so elegantly author the most important declaration of war on Blacks in our long history. Thus enshrining white supremacy, racism and inequality in perpetuity. All Nixon wanted to do was to sell out us American boys and ship us off to the Vietnamese Peninsula and mow down those gooks.

COLLEGE FOOTBALL

My real calling was football, and I was honored to be at UVA to play the game on full scholarship. I loved the calculus of running, throwing, and catching a cylinder shaped, leather wrapped, inflated rubber bladder across designated goal lines. How genius is that.

Played by two teams of eleven mean, fast, bone-crunching men, drugged out on steroids, amphetamines, and testosterone, going head-to-head for sixty endless minutes, in front national TV audiences and tens of thousands of screaming fans. Always on the verge of passing out or orgasming. Nothing like it.

As much as I loathe the game today, and instantly write off anyone who even comments about it, unless you're a Tom Brady fan, I still get an erection seeing a broken leg, a crushed knee or dangling fingers. Moreover, I can still cum to the sound of a concussion. It's pure bliss.

What a game. The high offset the breaks, headaches, and nightmares. And so what that 60% of all players, after five years or more, die at a young age from dementia, Alzheimer's, and other traumatic brain impairments?

At the time I reasoned, I could be in the jungles of Vietnam blowing off real human heads. College football was a mere video game in comparison.

You had to love it, especially when we played Army. Those losers, unlike today, had never smoked pot or done acid, and how easy it was to tell the difference between their players and ours. They saluted the flag. I stuck my finger up at it, as the rest of the team grabbed their groins.

LOWER CLASS KID

If you're wondering, I was a normal, well adjusted, lower class kid, that grew up for the first ten years of my life with my older brother in a thirty-foot trailer, hauled up and down the east coast of America from naval base to base, by parents, both veterans of the war. My Father was a Chief Petty Officer in the US Navy, who, after lying about his age, entered the war at seventeen and was promptly shipped overseas on an aircraft carrier.

My Grandfather, too, volunteered at nineteen to join the US Marine Corp, and was subsequently shipped to France to fight on the frontlines of WWI.

We were a proud disciplined military family and were told to eat all our food and sit up straight at breakfast, lunch, and dinner. Television was never allowed, nor was talking back.

I loved my dog and turtles and coloring books and baseball cards and obsessed over the game of chess and got straight A's all the way into high school. Until one night coming home drunk, with my best friend – a Native American and star quarterback, passed out in the backseat – I hit a telephone pole at high speed and went through the windshield of my Dad's new Chevy.

In a flash of shattered glass and blood, I went from

a hip and handsome sixteen-year-old surfer to a terrified broken Frankenstein. I couldn't recognize my head nor my identity. Both were mangled.

The trauma of the operation is still a recurring nightmare, with surgeons picking glass from my head and skull and then sewing it back together without anesthesia, for fear of not waking up.

Some friends who came to the Naval Hospital for a visit got so nauseous when they saw my bandaged head covered with thick dried blood that they ran to the washroom to throw up.

My face and eyes were so black and blue and swollen, I could not see nor walk for weeks, as both knees and chest were semi-crushed from slamming into the dashboard, with the rear of the engine in my lap. Of course, the seat belt was under my ass rather than around my waist.

A month later, I made it home with a walker and hundreds of thick stitches holding a reassembled head. Thus began the helter-skelter life of an undiagnosed TBI-T – traumatic brain injured teenager. And the beginning of a long opioid addiction, which metastasized into a fifty-year psychedelic, pharmaceutical and mindfulness addiction, simultaneously at that.

A TALK WITH GOD

Mid-way through my second year of college football, with near daily high impact head collisions and monthly concussions, I told my coach I was suffering and needed help. He sent me to a UVA counselor, who had a Ph.D. in keeping us kids indoctrinated. I explained my struggle: I was chronically dizzy, nauseous, fatigued, confused, impulsive, and couldn't sleep most nights, along with an increasing anxiety. I also told him I was drinking, smoking pot and cigarettes, and doing a lot of cocaine, especially on weekends after games.

He calmly explained, "Alan. Cut back on the drugs. You're a gifted athlete. You're smart and fast and you have great hands and moves. This pain is a small price to pay to become a professional player. Think of the money and the lifestyle of a pro. You're just two years away. Stay with it."

In looking back at that crossroads, what better therapy could there be for a traumatic brain injured teenager than to keep bashing his brain with 250-pound freight trains determined not only to tackle you but to ruin your life for good. Football, we were trained, is about permanently injuring the enemy and not just winning.

So, I just kept on keeping on. After all, the alternative, which I think the counselor knew, was blowing the heads off "the enemy" in Vietnam. Better to die of traumatic brain damage as a young man, rather than be ashamed for the rest of my life in giving up a college degree.

At least the migraines increased, which allowed me to keep my opioid addiction active. And to his credit, he did prescribe Valium and sleeping pills that allowed me for once to embody my Little Prince.

Finally, on the night of draft lottery in 1971, I dropped yet again another high dose of acid, and drove up to the Blue Ridge Mountains. I parked and walked a familiar path under the moon light with the Shenandoah Valley below. I found a spot and sat down, and had a heart to heart with my crossroads and God.

After a night of mindful reflection, I drove back to Charlottesville and, still high from the acid, formally returned my scholarship and withdrew from the life I could have led, to the life I was going to lead. Ultimately, it was not an easy decision, as one fork in the road pointed deeper into HELL and the other was merely red-hot coals.

LA AFTER ASIA

After an arduous and dangerous overland journey from France to India in 1976 and nearly two years of soul-searching throughout much of Asia, within a month of returning to America, I was living in the Hollywood Hills trying to figure out what's next. And in no time, the *Samsaric* emptiness echoed loudly, and I began to quiet the suffering, yet again, with cocaine, nicotine, opioids, alcohol, sex, and my greatest love of all – psycho-thera-peutically painting my mind on canvases often through-out the night.

When I cleared the attic after my Mom and Dad's

passing, I saw all these paintings from decades before, what was left of them. Art therapy on acid. ALL, self-portraits of despair.

All roads led back to that fundamental fact of Life: the Buddha's First Noble Truth of S.H.I.T. is – Suffering, Horror, Idiocy and Trauma. S.H.I.T. is a fact of life. S.H.I.T. is inherent in being alive. Nor could I simply wipe the S.H.I.T. from my mind.

If only at that crossroads there was a third road up the center – the MIDDLE PATH – avoiding extremes. But who can blame me or anyone? There was no local shaman in Hollywood at the time. No plant medicine guru. Nor an MDMA assisted psychotherapist on call for wayward young adults to excavate their unrecognized traumatic brain injury.

And so it was. Since Burma remained closed to foreigners, I, along with a few friends, invited Mahasi Sayadaw, the father of the worldwide lay mindfulness movement, to come to America to lead a few meditation retreats.

Ultimately, after two weeks at a Center in Southern California, and two more weeks at the Insight Meditation Society in Massachusetts, I had had enough of the American Scream and ordained as a Buddhist monk in New York City, and flew off the next day with my preceptor – Mahasi Sayadaw – to Burma.

At the time, Burma (now also known as Myanmar) was a little known South Asian country ravaged for 135 years by genocidal British imperialism. From that horror followed the brutality of World War II, and with it the country's urban centers – Rangoon, Mandalay and Moulmein – were carpet bombed by Allied forces to oust an invading fascist Japanese army.

Gaining its independence in 1947 from their white masters on Downing Street, Burma – all 17 million of them at that time – commenced for the next 74 years down a totalitarian road of BIG BROTHER dictatorships; each one becoming progressively more blood thirsty over the decades; sending tens of thousands of peaceful pro-democracy activists to gulags and labor camps, where the freedom-lovers were routinely tortured, raped, and tortured again and again and again.

In retrospect, I can hardly imagine I chose to leave LA to live in one of the most politically volatile, dangerous, and unhealthy environments in the world, and to find inner peace, no less. I was at that proverbial crossroads in life and every part of me yearned to learn this timeless practice of mindfulness meditation as taught by the Buddha, under the rare tutelage of Mahasi Sayadaw, one of the greatest meditation masters in the modern era.

For me, it was enlightenment or death. And my road was to BURMA, a totalitarian terror state ruled by General Ne Win – one of the most ruthless military dictators ever – who, to his credit, was merely acting out his trauma, healing, as it were, from decades of White British oppression while honing his inherited legacy of xenophobia, megalomania, and stress-free torture.

He was smart enough, however, to seal off his country from a new wave of foreign invaders and allowed visitors a maximum seven-day non-extendable stay permit. Although Burma was the most closed country in the world, I wanted in on her ancient Buddhism and moreover, on the power of meditation.

Sometimes, I do wonder if I had known what I know today, especially that extinction was upon us like a life-destroying asteroid hurtling towards our earthly abode at 85,000 MPH, might I have stayed in America and continued the defiant warrior's path, having fun slowly suffocating my spirit with drugs and sex and art and music and dancing, and, if lucky, being happily married and a celebrated film director as well.

I remember reflecting on the long flight to Burma – as a twenty-nine-year-old rebel novice going cold turkey on a daily cocktail of cocaine, opioids, Valium, sleeping pills and alcohol – that my ordination was nothing short of divine intervention.

Yes, if only I had had a good therapist at the time, I may have averted all those debilitating bouts of illnesses I would get in Burma; malaria, dengue, typhoid, cholera, dysentery and hepatitis. But think of how much you learned, Alan, living under a violent military dictatorship and seeing firsthand how many good people you knew were imprisoned and tortured. What a rare insight into the power of compassion and the evils of totalitarianism.

But looking back today, nothing would have stopped me. I was a traumatized moth flying headlong into the aspirational self and idealized flame of *Nirvana*.

BURMA: MY MONASTIC HOME

Arriving to Burma on a one-way ticket with a non-extendable seven-day visa – and with no precedent for an extension, ever – was by far the biggest challenge of my life. It was far bigger than giving up my six-year college scholarship, or facing my own ugliness and trauma from the car accident, or dealing with the murder of my best childhood friend. Nothing compared, other than facing the Abyss of Extinction.

At first it was a magic carpet ride. Upon arrival, thousands had gathered on the tarmac at the airport – chanting Buddhist hymns with candles lit in honor of my preceptor and teacher, Mahasi Sayadaw. The same along the seven-mile road to the monastery.

I thought I was on a different planet, other than the hyper-panic I was feeling from the withdrawals of going cold turkey on my addictions, along with the 100% humidity and torrid 104-degree heat.

Once at the monastery and given a small room, I was so desperate for cocaine and nicotine I snuck out a side gate of the center and asked a street vendor for a free cheroot – a special Burmese cigar laced with opium – that I knew about from my previous visit back in '77.

That night, I smoked every centimeter of that five-inch opiated blimp, until I lowered my head on a pillow-less cane mattress and went out into a stupor. Until the bell was rung at three am to get up and begin my life as a monk.

From day one, I was instructed to follow the twenty-hour a day retreat schedule of formal sitting and walking meditations, with only four hours of sleep, max. In addition, no speaking nor any solid food after twelve noon. And the dogs – fucking dogs everywhere; hundreds of them running around in packs, barking and fighting and fornicating day and night.

It felt like I had entered a prison camp.

If it wasn't for the butts of half smoked opiated cigars that I began to secretly pick up from an offbeat area of the monastery grounds where the day workers and kitchen staff hung out, I would have slit my wrists, or taken the entire vile of sleeping pills I brought with me, and rest in Buddhistic heaven.

As it turned out, the schedule was nothing compared to the hunger of not eating after 12 noon. But once I adjusted to voluntary starvation, the greater issue reared its head: SEX. It was mandatory: the absolute absence of the greatest joy and health producing activity known, intercourse.

No orifices allowed. NONE. Women. Men. Animals. Zip. All closed to fingers, tongues, toes, noses, ears, and penises, of course.

Monks are not even allowed to be in a room alone with a woman. Nor allowed to even insinuate the desire for sex or even intimacy. Not even mouthing a sexual sentence silently – I am so horny I am ready to die. I beg of you sister, please allow me to fantasize about your pussy. Nope. Nothing.

There was not even the relief of masturbation. That too was considered a grave offense. And if you think having no sex for a week or a month is tough, try going nearly four years without access to female orifices, and no masturbation either. As in none – ZERO. Close, but no banana.

As women have moon cycles, new monks have erection cycles. As the sexual repression intensified throughout the month, IT just grew and grew and grew in size for four or five or six days at a stretch.

You think Viagra creates a majestic unflinching stiffy, try spiritually inspired abstinence. It comes without a script and does not need to be ingested. All you must do is BELIEVE that fasting from sex and masturbation is the holiest thing a man or woman can do to access their inner Buddha.

You'd see some monks on day one of their erection cycle walking bent over to hide their thingie from poking out of their robes like a tent pole.

Day three; they would be seen eyeing nuns as they mindfully and slowly walked by them, as if they were in a nightclub looking to get laid.

Day four and five, some of the monks would be seen like they were hula-hooping but without the hula-hoop. Lost, as it were, in long slow circular motions with their waists.

In more extreme cases, you see some of the younger monks grinding trees. Others humping the bark smooth with sustained swirling rhythms. Even the woodpeckers would stop to watch, at times. And some of the dogs gathered and started to hump each other in solidarity.

I even once saw a monk wrestle himself to the ground, with one arm fighting the other to keep it off his dick. And every now and again, a monk would just disappear, and we'd hear later on that he had opened up a strip club in Patpong – the red-light district in Bangkok – needing to compensate for lost time in the monastery.

Little did I know how all pervasive the Buddha's First Noble Truth of S.H.I.T. really is. It was shitty in America and far shittier in Burma.

Going back to my room on day six, the only salvation was that I would be leaving in the morning, as it was the last legal day I could be in Burma. That is, unless it was extended. Which had never been done before to a non-diplomat or even a friend of the dictator.

My luck. With the taxi waiting to take me to airport,

I was told my visa had been EXTENDED. Thus began my career as a chronic mindfulness meditator.

MINDFULNESS IS ALL THERE IS

When you're a monk in a renowned meditation center practicing mindfulness, there's only one thing you do: PRACTICE MINDFULNESS. That's your career. All day. Everyday. And as much into the night as possible.

Where do you practice it? Take a guess? Project into the future? Dig into the past? Nope. Not for serious *yogis*. No escape allowed. ONLY RIGHT HERE and RIGHT NOW, and as many nows that follow, until you die. And trust, me, there are a lot of NOWS in the day.

By comparison, your typical day in the life of a well-adjusted Western mindfulness practitioner generally goes from wake up, caffeinate, do a bit of *yoga* and listen to a podcast, do a Zoom session or two to cover the rent, have lunch, masturbate, low dose, a bit of sacred porn, see your girlfriend, have wine and dinner, have sex, watch a show on Netflix, fight, have a shot of Scotch, makeup, and repeat.

In a monastery, you have twenty hours of NOWS without a break. If you're counting, that's a NOW a SECOND. For those quick at math, that's sixty NOWS a minute. 3,600 NOWS an hour. Multiple that by a mandatory eight hours of sitting meditation NOWS a day. That's 28,800 NOWS, in sitting meditation alone.

Of course, nows don't just happen in one posture or every now and again. Those fuckers are unrelenting, as in there's always a Now, whether you like it or not.

Like Covid, NOWS are everywhere; they stalk you in all POSTURES; sitting, standing, walking, pooing, bathing, lying down, eating, every goddamn thing you do has a NOW attached to the crossroads.

There are no time outs from NOWS. Even when you're daydreaming. The damn NOW is unashamed of your unmindfulness. NOW is there whether you like it or not.

I often reflected on how I gave up a six-year scholarship and a possible shot at the Presidency for a life of NOWS.

You learn fast as a monk that you made a COLLOSAL mistake in meditating, as in full time and open ended. You even think you put yourself in the worse possible situation on Earth. A mindfulness prison. Or a labor camp where the punishment is to do NOTHING other than be MINDFUL. No other work allowed; no phone, no texting, no music, no Netflix, no sex, no books, no podcasts, no day trading, nothing. Only you and the NOW. And in silence, no less. Talking with your now is not even allowed.

I really wondered at times if this mindfulness thing was a cruel joke. All for what, to be more efficient, productive, present in the NOW?

Over and over again you hear teachers tell you,

there is no activity TOO INCIDENTAL not to be mindful of: at all TIMES, all CIRCUMSTANCES, all STATES, all CONTEXTS at each of the SIX SENSE DOORS. Be mindful.

BE mindful from the moment you become aware you are awake in the morning, right up until you take your very last breath before you go to sleep at night. BE MINDFUL.

You are often asked on what breath did you wake up on in the morning? Was it the in breath or out breath and where exactly in the process were you? And moreover, what did you see and what did you learn in the process? And the same when falling asleep.

TWENTY HOURS A DAY, ALL DAY, every day, just one thing: BE MINDFUL, RIGHT NOW.

REFLECTING ON THE JOURNEY

In looking over the five decades of my mindful life and the millions of choices at the crossroads of each year – it's a split screen of both awe and horror; a Buddhist-oriented kaleidoscope of mystical adventure, with drug-inspired epiphanies and trauma-inducing pitfalls. Along with way too many years of intensive meditation and a defense system that even moment-to-moment mindfulness, MDMA-assisted psychotherapy, and decades of anti-depressants couldn't penetrate.

I'm also reminded of the meaninglessness of legacy when LIFE is no more; with my troves of hard drives and near endless files of long forgotten letters and photographs and memories that will all disappear.

There are, however, highlights I'm proud of: eleven books, endorsements by eight Nobel laureates, including President Jimmy Carter and Congressman Tom Lantos – a survivor of Auschwitz; a feature documentary on my life story; a Hollywood film I helped script that followed the story line of one of my books; another film I was hired to write on the 'meaning of love in the time of genocide,' that brought me to the former Yugoslavia for the final year of their war; a long career as a maverick *dharma* teacher; a satirical solo-performer with nearly 200 shows; a journalist in areas of war and conflict; volunteered in refugee camps; was up close to guerrilla war and genocide; and even managed a few insights along the way that seemed, at the time, to pierce the veil of my confusion.

Even thought I was enlightened for a spell, until I finally realized what I was saying and how I was living were inconsistent. And no matter how I tried to close the gap, the joy of the double life got the better of me.

On the one hand, back in the day I was rock star meditation teacher – one of the first in the West leading retreats and groups with movie moguls, celebrities, and some of America's spiritual elite. And on the one hand, enjoying, yet again, a range of risky behaviors, with drugs, alcohol, cigarettes; and most enjoyable were the Osho

Rajneesh sex workers – the world's best and spiritually incorrect enough to have mercy on me – to reintroduce an evangelical rebel Buddhist meditation teacher to my sacred *Shiva-lingum* again, after a spell of bone-chilling monastic celibacy.

When I returned to America in the early eighties, after having been thrown out of Burma by the dictator, for the third time, believing, I was told, that I was a bogus underground monk working for the CIA, my life was flipped upside down, yet again.

A THERAPIST IN MARIN

After years as a celibate non-masturbating monk, I wasn't horny per se, as in ready to hump any orifice encased in skin or fur, dead or alive. I was both excited and frozen, having forgotten, if you will, what it actually meant to touch my own thingie again. And moreover, to fondle a breast and even two at time. Or to suck a nipple.

It was beyond me to integrate the conflicting desire for sex with the repulsion for it. To actually relearn this simplest of things: how to put my sacred beloved finger in that slithery pink thingie down there, where pee pee and blood and all kinds of other fluids come out.

Why would I want to relearn how to do that, I thought? OMG! And further, to lower my head between a woman's legs, as if I was putting on a fleshy life preserver, and put my face and tongue in her fleshy wet thingie. It better be shaved I thought. No way was I going to mimic the behavior of a monastic beaver.

At the time, I couldn't even say the word pussy, much less touch him down there and deliberately conjure up sexual fantasies sufficient enough to make him stiff and shoot tooth paste everywhere.

There was a time however, even when I was seven years old, that I could masturbate proudly and with stealth and do it again and again. Even did it on the school bus and a few times in class with my hand in my pocket, fantasizing about my hot second grade teacher.

Strange, the power of meditation to turn one away from their healthy pursuits – life, love, intimacy, sex, wealth, status, power and all other perversities and self-destructive addictions – of a normal well-adjusted former Buddhist monk. Leave it to thinking you are enlightened to truly fuck up your life.

I thought being a monk was difficult. Nothing is more traumatic than being a former monk, a Westerner at that, and attempting to integrate back into the world. And I would assume the same is true for a woman.

You think giving up smoking is difficult? Or cocaine or heroin or Oxycontin? Or narcissism? Or hating Donald Trump for that matter? Try giving up celibacy.

I mean, just look at how adept the Catholic Church is in preserving both the sanctity and sanity of their monks' celibacy. They don't waste time with leaving the monastic order first to pursue a life of healthy consensual sex. No. They keep their vows, learn to lie to themselves and each other, and act out their sexuality in secret; grooming boys and girls over decades to let the Holy Priests worship at the altar of their orifices and purge them from their sins.

Unlike Buddhist monasteries, in all my years in Burma, never heard of a monk or nun even masturbating, much less having sex. In hindsight, it's clearly due to the repressive power of meditation and mindfulness. That damn stuff is effective.

In your early years, meditation acts like novocaine to numb one's most basic human functions. As you develop in depth and insight, especially if you OCD on mindfulness as I did, it has the potential to lobotomize your sex drive, as well as your lust for money, power and privilege. It's no wonder why Burma is dominated by military dictators. They are non-meditators and the majority of the people are mindfulness practitioners.

As for me, I knew I needed professional help to come back into my body and re-enter my relationship with women. When I really let it in, I knew that a perfectly adept sex worker was one thing to help my healing, and they did to a large part, but if I were to truly heal and get to the root of this issue, I had to face that I had serious problem and to not waste time in starting a Celibacy Anonymous program.

No, Alan, seek California's finest sex therapist.

So, after asking for help among fellow teachers, who said it was beyond them to know how to assist, other than recommit to the five Buddhist precepts, and refusing to call Tara – my beloved sex worker at the Osho escort service in Mill Valley – I did an MDMA assisted psychotherapy session that convinced me that I had to face this problem head on, or I would act out with my followers.

Searched the yellow pages and found a psychiatrist with amazing testimonials, who, to my surprise specialized in bringing back to life enlightened Western mindfulness meditation teachers just back from their arduous trainings in Asia.

Her statement of purpose was what sold me: "I am here to reintroduce you to the power of the pussy while snapping you from the trance of enlightenment and taking you to new dimensions of self-realization."

I said, "WTF?" My learning to trust that 'quiet voice within' from all those years of ardent meditation practice was paying off.

I called and took her up on her free one-hour session to see if we were a fit.

I showed up at my appointed time and learned that Shakti-Ma had a Ph.D. from the California Institute of Integral Studies in Transformational Mindfulness Assisted Sex Therapy for Former Buddhist Monks and Western *Vipassana* Teachers.

Besides being a stunner, Shakti-Ma explained that her motivation to help her clients was born from her many years of stripping as a young woman at a high-end sex club in downtown San Francisco.

Later, she moved to Hong Kong and was employed at an elite $1000 an hour escort agency servicing wealthy businessmen and celebrities passing through the city. Throughout those years, besides being flown all over the world, becoming rich, and knowing the entitled male psyche like none other, she realized "just how difficult it was for men to truly know how to touch and make love with a woman."

"Alan, you'd be surprised at how ignorant men are in understanding the mind and heart and body of a real woman," she explained.

"No, I get it," I replied. "I think I'm stuck somewhere around fourteen when I got hooked on masturbating to Penthouse magazine cover girls."

"That's right, Alan, most men go back ever further and are frozen in time."

"It was only after I returned to the States," she continued, "and began working at Kittens in the City that I also started to attend a Monday night meditation class in Oakland. My heart opened while listening to a former monk speak so beautifully and compassionately about his addiction to prostitutes during his stint in the Peace Corp. And later, how he folded even more by compensating for a sexless marriage by hiring sex workers here at the Osho Escort Branch in San Rafael. His moral courage was breathtaking.

"Sadly, he explained with tears, his wife discovered his transgressions and left him. And later, a colleague of his was my client and explained how this same man had a mental breakdown during a small teacher gathering, while sharing how his wife excoriated him in a therapy session that "all you want is harder, faster, deeper, and then turn over and put it in my ass. And you call yourself a meditation teacher and moralize to everyone else about coming from the heart? What else have you lied about? At least Trungpa was up front. You're among the biggest hypocrites the West has ever seen."

"His colleague said that when he shared his crisis in the group, he broke down and wept like a baby.

"But sadly, I later heard through another of his colleagues that he went back to his old ways and moved over to the Osho Escort Service in Mill Valley and met a woman named Tara. Perhaps you know her.

"Regardless, his dilemma convinced me to pursue my own true calling and stop lying to myself.

"Then when I saw how mindfulness was taking off around the world and how much money these fraudulent teachers were making with their inflated Asian trainings and flimsy Ph.D.'s, I thought there must be so many other men with the same problem as that former monk.

"Thus began my genuine spiritual life," she affirmed.

Soon after she explained that she abandoned her sex worker life and went back to college, eventually going on to medical school, and from there trained as a psychiatrist. And not just some ordinary shrink. She specialized in the shadow side of not only men's sexuality but "highly spiritual men" like me, "successful meditation teachers with large followings and bestselling books."

A few, she said, although she was discrete not to disclose names, had meditation centers, and some were so compartmentalized and cunning that they could teach the ancient practice of *metta* or loving kindness meditation to large groups, and later that night go to Kittens and hire a girl for a few hours.

As she explained, she wanted to help these well intended super-stars from becoming spiritual frauds and hypocrites, and, if they were already suffering from narcissism, to come out of the closet and realign with their moral integrity and live a much more whole and honest life with their partners or wives, and most of all with their students.

She encouraged me that I was right to be catching my inner fraudster early in my career.

She went onto explain that, for most successful teachers, once the addiction takes root, although they are good at loving other people, they struggle with loving themselves. As such, they act out, often violating their students, and in some cases, even forcing them to have sex with them while other students watch.

"Some even go so far as to tell them that it was a special teaching designed specifically for their *dharma* development. Others coerce them into bringing their girlfriends in for group practice. Hopeless at that point. I call it "excessive meditation syndrome" and "delusional enlightenment disorder." If together, generally untreatable.

"Most of these men know they shouldn't be teaching but the money is good and the sex is plentiful. I know, I was there once and trust me, being a high paid sex worker is not all that bad. It's not an easy addiction to break. But I did.

"I will say in all honesty, the men you meet as a high-end escort are far more interesting than these spiritual teacher types. I know, you are an exception, that's way I'll consider you as a client."

She then closed the session by explaining how the only true healing was to act out one's sexual fears and fantasies in the sanctity and safety of THE HEALER'S OFFICE. "Here we save *Sanghas* from collapsing," she said. "We also save needless years in court in litigation and lawsuits with students."

"Trust me," she concluded, "doing whatever you want with my body for $350 an hour for five sessions is well worth the savings of five years of weekly psychotherapy, the anti-depressants and in many cases the long addiction to costly untrained escorts to play out your fantasies. But it's your call. Nip the addiction in the bud or risk hiding and lying as your success builds."

"If you're wondering," she explained, "I do have boundaries. I don't do violence. I like to slap and be spanked. But no ropes, masks, or whipping." I assured her I was ordinary.

"You'd be surprised," she continued, "how many spiritual teachers love to be paddled and some even like to crawl on all fours with a collar and leash and be called by their monk's name. One wonders what goes down in those Asian monasteries. But it's probably more to do with their need for fame to overcome their inadequacy issues."

She then invited me to begin the process, saying, "Let's get started with you sharing some of your recurring sexual fantasies. And when you speak do so mindfully please, and slowly and feel each word and the energy inherent in them.

"And while you speak, I am going to undress and sit in front of you and touch myself. While you watch, imagine seeing me with the same reverence you feel for a *Buddha* statue that sits in front of the meditation hall when you are leading a retreat. And include yourself as well in that same field of loving kindness."

"Nope, not me," I told her. Too intimate. Too real.

After she gave me her card, I thanked her and went

on about my way. Just carried on with integrating my life in the best way I knew how; mindful REPRESSION and mindful DENIAL and those beloved Osho sex workers that never suggested for a minute there was something to heal. "Just be yourself," Tara always said. "From there all truth will be revealed."

"And remember this, Alan," Tara said with her trademark wit, "repression is one of the finest of spiritual paths, as it allows you to bury your duplicity and cover it with humorous storytelling, moralizing and feigned compassion for the masses. When in doubt, give me a call," she concluded with a laugh.

WILD WILD COUNTRY

I love you, *Osho Rajneesh*, for training Tara so well, but after watching your Netflix Special, "Wild Wild Country," I wasn't down with the mass poisoning of the good folks in Antelope, Oregon. But on the other hand, how skillful of you to inspire a new generation of sleazy Western drug dealers to turn from their lowly work and take up the hustling of hyper-commercialized tantra, breathwork, and the only true path of love and intimacy.

Yet, crazy me, I admit, of all spiritual books, I love reading Osho's the most. Especially his MDMA-driven "Diaries of a Madman." I can so relate. In all honesty, it's one of my greatest unrealized visions: to have a Patron donate a well-stocked private ocean-side mansion for my remaining years with an endless supply of organic ecstasy, high quality acid, mushrooms, and DMT, and my genius mystical lover and I wake every morning to do *yoga*, take a walk on the beach, drink a fresh juice, then press video record to erotically *ubuntify* together about the nature of love and freedom and existential rebellion. And repeat every other day. What a great vision!

The other irony, despite my long association with Buddhism and insight meditation, is that Buddhists, and especially "enlightened teachers," oddly make the worst of friends. Never realized what a cut-throat business Buddhism was until I entered the fray after leaving Burma back in the day.

Rather than having open-hearted, dynamic, mutually supportive *dharma* colleagues, it was more like a clash of Mafia bosses. Cross the line, try to take any of our key students, outsize my retreats, get more donations than I do, talk to one of my Patrons or ghost writers, hit on any of my favorites fuck bunnies, break ranks with any of our lies, question our pharmaceutical drug use or our enlightenment, or our lust for fame and money and favor, or God-forbid cease colluding with our double life, and we'll mindfully cancel you and ruin your reputation, permanently. One mean competitive bunch.

Whereas with Osho trained followers, and I have so many of them as dear brothers and sisters, despite many of them being hustlers, frauds and thieves, they are loyal, caring, intelligent, self-deprecating, funny and generous. And I don't just mean *tantra* trained escort workers. I'm talking serious meditators, and some of the most astute psychologists and relationship coaches on Earth. Love them.

But to my bewilderment, I ran into an elite Osho trained priestess in Hawaii recently who passionately explained how "Wild Wild Country" was "pure bullshit." The truth is, "Osho not only knew everything about the mass poisoning in Antelope, he orchestrated it."

She went onto explain how the Guru called the commune his "Mystical Theater" and his "ultimate play of Oneness." And often referred to his creation as "the Master's great mockery of duality."

Further, "Osho even satirized God and the inherent evil of religion itself, by placing his unsuspecting throngs of brainwashed actors under surveillance, and further, training them as existential combatants to use automatic rifles and go into cosmic battle with the local white supremacists. You could say he was a mystical Shakespeare with the skill of a Peter Brook in producing Existential Theater.

"Meanwhile, he mocked even his most intimate followers by showing them how easily they would dutifully relinquish their own wealth and inheritances by giving it to the Great Master. To shine back, of course, his gratitude with his fleet of 46 Rolls Royce's, helicopter guns ships, and a private jet fueled and with a pilot ready to flee. As Osho did, and was stopped, jailed and assumed murdered by poisoning by the global elites."

The only religious people who have given Osho's sociopathic cunning and perversity a run for his money are the elite Tibetan Buddhist Teachers, the advanced South American "plant medicine" healers, the most enlightened *Yoga* and Hindu Masters, and of course, the Catholic priests get the Academy Award for their decades-long grooming campaign of making 'All Children Matter.'

But it must be stated, the Hindus of India, like Osho himself, have a way of attracting the most intelligent sexy Western women in the world. Makes you almost want to become a *yoga* teacher just be around such succulent *yoni*.

A SECRET SAINT IN INDIA

After travelling Asia in the mid-70s, including Sri Lanka, Ladhk and Burma, I felt more disconnected from life than ever. Even sacred India was a turn off, with its rancid mix of misogynist men cherishing cows more than women, and a guru class of con artists and other sleazy predator types with their hustler Western students undergoing wannabe *yoga* teacher trainings. And throw in the air pollution, traffic congestion, mosquitoes, diarrhea, and near constant nausea; give me Bali any day.

Regardless, something kept drawing me back to the Motherland and the birthplace of Buddhism in 6 BC. One of the more interesting experiences I had, just before *yoga* and meditation became brands, was a fortuitous meeting with a secret Indian saint in the ancient city of Benares.

While hanging at the Burning Ghats one night along the River Ganges, lost in watching the fire burn back the skin of a beautiful Indian woman like filo-dough, an Indian man asked me if I would like to be the first Westerner to meet a soon-to-be-celebrity Saint. Of course, I responded, far better than another night reflecting on death, attempting to drop my attachment to youth and beauty.

After a short walk we entered a lantern-lit rock-walled cavern. There I was introduced to a handsome young Indian man named *Sri Smutagyi*, or simply SMUT, as he preferred to be called.

"The SMUT lineage," SMUT explained, "came from a long line of descended spiritual masters who specialized in sexual healing." SMUT said that they not only embodied the sacred teachings of *Patanjali's* Eight Limbs of *Yoga*, but innovatively added a ninth limb called, "*yoni* pole *yoga*," or just "*yoni yoga*," as SMUT preferred.

"In breaking with ancient Indian tradition, the head of the lineage was not a man," SMUT continued, "but a bisexual woman. Further, she's not even Indian. Rather, she's an American and a supporter of Joe Biden.

"In addition, she's Black: a Black Bi-Goddess," SMUT

said. "And she's so pure that she does not even realize that in her previous life she was a Being of Light in a higher celestial realm – and her ROLE was that of being the BI-tantra teacher to *Maitreya*.

"YES", he said. "Mai, the next Buddha to be, is both a woman and BI. You probably know her Alan," SMUT said with a tone of reverence. "Her name is Cardi B – the American hip hop artist. And we refer to her respectfully as *Sri-Cardi-B-Gyi* or in short, Sri W.A.P. Or, Her Holiness – with the Wet Ass Pussy."

SMUT went onto explain that "Sri WAP is an underground saint and only known to his own secret circle of Indian male teachers who are training in "*yoni* pole *yoga* sexual healing therapy for Western women."

"Uniquely, to avoid predation and re-traumatizing the women, our men are GAY. We train them to channel Sri WAP's healing essence, in order for them to cure what's known as W.A.S.P. – or wet ass spiritual pussy disorder. And the more advanced form of *yoni* trauma called X–W.A.S.P., or excessively wet ass spiritual pussy disorder.

"Apparently the excessive wetness," SMUT explained, "is due to the historical trauma of the woman in not having healthy sex early enough in their life. Ideally, under fifteen years old is best.

"Normally, here in the Motherland," he continued, "we see our girls ready for fornication by about eleven or twelve years old at the latest. By thirteen or fourteen she gives head like a veteran. But we understand that Western spiritual women are somewhat behind the transformational curve.

"See, the completion of our 'W.A.S.P. therapy certification program' is meant to liberate the wetness of the Western women's *yoni* from historical toxins, and other cancer creating chemicals, not only from the lack of proper sex at an early age but also from carnivore-based diets. Especially diets comprising of free-range chicken, hook and line caught tuna, and grass fed ethically killed beef.

"Our '*yoni* pole *yoga*' gay teachers," he concluded, "will soon travel the world to service the tens of thousands of *yoga* centers and its twenty-billion-dollar *yoga* industry. And I may add, unlike South American plant medicine shamans, who I'm told give miserable cunnilingus, our Indian teachers are the best.

"Last but not least, since our teachers are gay, they are doing a special service for the white women. When our teachers are giving the women oral sex to see that they have a healthy orgasm, they imagine it's a man's anus, and not her *yoni*. Ethics are everything, so our teachers are trained to keep well defined boundaries.

"And for the climax of the W.A.S.P. sexual healing process, our beloved gay teachers force themselves to strap on dildos to demonstrate to our beloved Western women clients just how sacred sex should be practiced with their true-life partners. During this final purification process the women chant *Sir-Cardi-B-Gyi's* famous Goddess poem to the tune of "*Om nama Shivia*." Please chant along with me Alan and then we can have some Chai Tea.

Yeah, you fucking with some wet-ass *yoni-yoga* pussy
Bring a bowl and a mop for this *yoni*-pole pussy
Give me all you've got to slurp my dripping wet pussy
Eat it up, *yogi*, catch a charge
Extra large and extra hard
Put this pussy right in your face
Swipe your tongue like a gold credit card
Hop on top, I wanna ride your rock
Spit your love in my mouth, look in my eyes
This pussy got wet only for you, come take a dive
Tie me up until I'm hot and neutralized
Let's role play, I'll wear *Mara's* mask
I want you to park that big meat truck
Right inside this tight wet garage
Make me cream, make me scream
I'm healed now with a new spiritual pussy

"Thank you for your visit, Alan. This is our small contribution to the spread of our sacred system of *yoga* around the world. We even hope to have some Lou-Lou-Lemon *yoni*-pole-*yoga* Ambassadors soon. Along with our very own "spiritual gangsta" clothing line and "bad ass" *yoga* wear. All in due time, of course.

"Yes, some call it compassion in action. But in our language, Alan, we call it, *"yoni yoga* off the mat." After a long pause SMUT concluded with a wry smile. "Or 'back on her mat *yoga*', and occasionally, "her face and knees too." Wink wink, SMUT twinkled with a grin.

THE BLACK HOLE OF DENIAL

I paused in MY journey and went to the washroom to mindfully purge. And after recommitting to self-honesty, I reflected on how easy it is to lie to ourselves. Thinking, how good folks who are in DENIAL about their DENIAL, so often, willfully perpetuate their DENIAL through spiritual practices, especially meditation, *yoga* and mindfulness. Whereas MOST who TEACH such practices unknowingly reinforce DENIAL both in themselves and their students. Thus, the teaching of self-honesty becomes the Big Brother art of self-deception and spiritual propaganda.

To state the obvious, mindfully masking one's shadow has become big business and those who obsess over their so-called "Special Awakening" project their grandiosity by either DOING or TEACHING – yet another *satsang*, yet another authenticity circle, yet another ten-day *Vipassana* retreat, yet another purging, yet another trauma release. Yet another, yet another... All for what? To live more fraudulently in yet another masked moment, in order to teach others to live more passionately in yet another mindful moment of embodied DENIAL.

It's somewhat perverse and ironic both, how the mind 'mindfully' denies the truth in the moment, to practice being mindful of the NOW, in order to discover the truth that is denied in the previous moment. Said in another way, the NOW becomes the black hole for denial, and with that it spews out a whole host of "spiritual disorders."

Of course, as one matures in their DENIAL and SELF-DECPTION by being unmindful of the LIE in Being – PRESENT – critical thinking, reflective reasoning and ethical doubt recedes. And if one practices long and deep enough, integrity vanishes altogether down the rabbit hall of pathological hypocrisy.

It is therefore not surprising that many self-pro-claimed enlightened Buddhist mindfulness teachers have undiagnosed DTS-L – Trump Derangement Syndrome Lite – as well as the more advanced sociopathy, Globalist Grandiosity Syndrome, or simply, follow the money or SELL-OUT Syndrome.

SATI – the only word for mindfulness in the origi-nal *Pali* Buddhist literature – literally means "memory" – clear, comprehensive and courageous recollection and reflection on what was, and NOT merely bare attention of ONLY NOW.

Why the reluctance to employ the power of mind-fulness, I wondered, as radical self-honesty that includes transparency both about the present and the past – lies and all.

And so it's no wonder, I reasoned, in full view of the morphine on the table in front of me, that here we are heading mindfully blind or "blindfully" into the Abyss.

The urgency of the reflection compelled me to engage in my own mindful recollection to glean neglected insights, feel buried hurts, uncover repressed passions, unmask hypocrisies, let go of shame and hesitancy, elevate hidden strengths, and most of all look for solutions to the climate emergency – AND, if possible, to rise UP and, despite the odds, manifest ACTS of CONSCIENCE, however small they may be.

The crossroads of today was clear: hell or hope; life one way, death the other. Or, life and death one way, and a little life and a very bad death the other.

D.E.A.D SYNDROME

Back in America during my reentry period, I learned quickly that meditation and much of Buddhism, especially if you went deep in your practice, didn't mix. How often I felt that it would have been far better to have left the "practice" back in the country from where it had come, and adjust to an entirely new set of hybrid "world *dharma*" teachings and practices in the location you've landed.

Be forewarned: the timeless transformation teachings

and the insights gained in the East, especially if enlightened, CANNOT BE INTEGRATED.

Despite popular brainwashing about 'meditation off the cushion' and '*yoga* off the mat', and psychotherapy off the flatscreen, and plant medicine off the toilet, and Zoloft out of the vile, save yourself decades of therapy: ASIAN-BASED INSIGHTS CANNOT BE INTEGRATED into real life. If you try, you will suffer, and badly, despite having a lot of fun and possibly getting rich and famous in the process.

It has been my experience that one's "timeless truths" vanish like a toilet swallows poo. Your enlightenment is mangled like a garburator does scraps. Wisdom is a misnomer for glorified self-deception. Authenticity a cover for narcissism. Truth-telling is doublespeak for lying. Discovering the true nature of consciousness is a lame cover for capitalism. Freedom just a poor excuse for consumerism. And your workshops and retreats become "gigs" under the guise of sacred events.

At first, I was baffled by this counter-intuitive realization. As in, was my dysfunction prior to enlightenment so dysfunctional that it took a perfectly good enlightenment and ate it for lunch? Or perhaps I got a bogus *Nirvana*? Or was my awakening a placebo that has worn off? Were my *dharma* teachers social scientists in disguise, working underground for an AI start up? Why did I feel so displaced? Why was everything not as it should be?

In truth, behaviors that one was supposed to have overcome – post-enlightenment – I did with greater frequency than before enlightenment. Did them even more so than during my drug dealing years in school.

As a *dharma* teacher, I wasn't selling drugs anymore (although I know several who have) or stashing away stacks of cash as a drug cartel member would (and I have known those who teach and did that as well), but I was doing more drugs than ever before and equally attached to "quantities." As in the number of *yogis* at retreats, the amount of donations received, and both the quality and quantity of invitations to speak or teach. Nor were the amounts ever enough. More *yogis*, more donations, more opportunities, more celebrity – more was always better.

Why such a discrepancy before and after, I wondered?

Even little things changed: Stopped smoking for the final three years as a monk; started again after enlightenment. Stopped drinking, now drinking more than ever, and only high end whiskey at that. Was comfortable before in cheap Indian garb; designer threads only now. Had a cheap car before, why the need for a leased Mercedes? Stopped looking at Penthouse when I entered high school, and now I had it delivered monthly. Cut my own hair pre-India, now only the best stylist in Mill Valley. Ate vegetarian at cool funky spaces before Burma, now only meat dishes at ritzy 4- & 5-star restaurants in whatever city I was in. Had a steady relationship prior to ordination, now all I considered were models, sex workers, and movie stars. And short term only.

Something wasn't right.

Was I alone? No. With all the meditation and mindfulness practiced everywhere over the past fifty years, the world has only gotten worse. Not one person I know has broken free from the "cult of extinction." Nor declared war on their *Sangha's* complicity with the "homicidal economy." Why? Why has there been fifty years of mindfulness and the world has only gotten worse? And me too. What am I missing?

I imagined AA claiming success in overcoming alcoholism while compensating with a crack fetish. Well, there may be some wisdom to that. At least one gives up slurring words, angry fights, and hangovers, for a clear mind, weight loss, and rapid speech.

See, when I returned to the West and began to teach, I thought the integration of my Enlightenment would simply enhance all things good. Little did I know how good it would become. Little did I know that I developed the highly coveted post enlightenment realization called the 'double life.'

Good teachers work hard to acquire this skill. And it does not come easily. You must first realize that you are suffering from the denigrating neuroplasticity of excessive meditation that metastasizes into a permanent brain disorder called, "Delusional Enlightenment Authenticity

Dyslexia," or D.E.A.D, as it will soon be described in the expanded edition of the "Diagnostic and Statistical Manual of Mental and Spiritual Disorders" used by mental health professionals and well-trained meditation teachers.

The symptoms of this rare condition are nuanced. Successful Western *dharma* teachers especially, and some Eastern ones as well, will know this: If you are a little white liar before enlightenment, you become an aggressive cunning scoundrel afterwards. If you were only slightly greedy before your great awakening, afterwards you become Trump-like in your obsession for wealth, status, and privilege. If you had a somewhat healthy sex life before the big E, you become either a sex addict with a porn addiction and/or develop an escort service habit, and/or treat your retreats like a singles bar for servicing your sexual and other greed-based needs.

And as for more advanced *dharma* teachers, they develop eating disorders and either become obese or anorexic, as I did, and hide their lies behind a *metta*-fetish and/or faux-enlightenment obsession, and advocate to their students how, on the one hand, they eat mindfully with strangers, but when home alone, or with complicit friends, binge like their life depended on it.

Sadly, so-called truly good spiritual friends are the last to tell you the truth about yourself. And if they do, they're OUT.

Collusion is the real *Sangha* in the West and the

Guiding Teachers Guild is really a collusive oligarchy and a euphemism for authoritarianism to maintain privilege, profit, and brand control.

Now, if you become super successful at your spiritual craft, your entitlement factor goes through the roof. And for many, I'm told, they think that every woman that attends their retreats, certainly the most attractive, sexiest and wealthiest, have come specifically to have sex with you and/or to bestow upon you their riches.

The full fruition of enlightenment disorder kicks in when one reaches near fatal levels of D.E.A.D. Syndrome. One literally goes numb inside and they start to believe their own lies.

In these more psychotic levels of the disorder, teachers are known to have flowers thrown on their footpath as they walk to the front of the room and insist that students bow when addressing them or sitting nearby. They often fly in private planes or, when slumming it, go First Class and never lower than Business. They attend SPIRITUAL ELITE only parties (known as S-ELITES) and scoff at anyone who may be there without big followings and bestselling books, EVEN IF you are a stunner with perfect everything.

Of course, S-ELITES often have a fulltime ghost writer, and a social media team to promote their I-ME-MINE *dharma* brand. They are also surrounded by sycophants who clean their homes and toilets and see exactly how neurotically self-obsessive they are. But being so entranced with the lie of one's beloved teacher and his or her so-called "LIFE-CHANGING AWAKENING," students suck it up and dine for another sycophantic day on sublimated crow. And in time, learn to bury their perceptions for fear of being estranged or worse yet, thrown out and labeled a "traumatized abuser."

This special class of Western spiritual elitism often comes with the Hindu-holy suffix "GYI" placed by oneself at the end of their re-appropriated Hindu name. Whereas for Buddhists, the equivalent of GYI is Ph.D., supplemented with ghost writers, editors, publicist, personal assistant, a driver, personal accountant, social media team, house cleaner, Hedge Fund broker, sex workers, and of course, a compulsory hatred of Donald Trump, while denying how they themselves got hijacked by a Me First Capitalist Crusade.

Until you reach the highest stage of Awakened (BOGUS ENLIGHTENMENT) Integration and have mastered the art of mindfully erasing all transgressions from one's memory. Now the double life has been fully liberated and you are an Awakened highly trained spiritual cyborg. You have transcended self-identity. You are truly emptiness hollowed of real. Authenticity perfected. AKA brainwashed by one's own narcissistic BS.

Now you can be truly proud of your masterful

fraudulence, memorized riffs, precision protected double life, and your vault of sacred lies and secrets, and confidently go on to the 2nd, 3rd and even 4th stages of enlightenment. And proudly carry on the HOLY lineage of "DO AS I SAY, NOT AS I DO." The enlightenment meme for Brain D.E.A.D. Anonymous.

It's no wonder, I thought, why so many spiritual and Buddhist teachers hate Donald J. Trump. He triggers their own un-owned Trump-ism.

OWN YOUR OUTRAGE

An alert on my iPhone broke me from reflection and centered me at the crossroads of either choosing 'life' and a call to action or 'death' through mindful euthanasia and on to my next life.

When it beeped again, I looked down through the eyes of the acid and read the New York Times Breaking News Alert: "Joe Biden has been declared the winner of the US presidential election."

My God, I gasped. How is it possible? Both candidates were bad burlesque, but Biden? Like all of America, we went to sleep last night and Trump was far ahead and in all the battleground states. It was a guaranteed win. A fraudulent election? Could it be so? Was the Wuhan bio-virus a cover for a deep state takeover?

Everyone who respects the "truth" in politics knows the courageous journalism of Glenn Greenwald, who broke the story of Edward Snowden's Global Surveillance Disclosure. I remembered the SHOCK I felt reading Greenwald's article: THE REAL SCANDAL: U.S. MEDIA USES FALSEHOODS TO DEFEND JOE BIDEN FROM HUNTER'S EMAILS (found on his "hard drive from HELL").

Glenn CUTS through the lies of the corporate media, allowing decades of evidence to reveal the Biden Syndicate to be morally vacuous agents of Wall Street, profiteers of "America's forever wars," and moreover, IN BED with America's greatest ENEMY – the genocidal nuclear-armed Communist Party of China.

On the other hand, Dangerous Donald is insufferable with his personality flaws, but to have a neoliberal follow the money globalist sell-out in the White House for four years is the Great Reset on crack and a fast track towards technocratic Totalitarianism. This must be an imperialist corporate coup, I thought. Or is it the genocidal dictator of China, Xi Jinping's communist inspired scam, eyeing the world as their next Tibet? *Samsara* just got darker. The house was now burning like never before.

I looked down at the morphine and heard the Doomsday Clock ticking in my head. This is indeed an existential nightmare. As Isaiah proselytized, "Woe to those who call evil good and good evil, who put darkness for light and light for darkness, who put bitter for sweet and sweet for bitter."

Has the BIG LIE just begun? Blame your ENEMY, then CANCEL them? Are we as good as dead, I wondered? Am I next on the block?

I turned off the phone, took a long slow mindful breath and listened for Bob's guidance and there he was: "The fight is far from over, Alan. DO NOT GIVE UP. Own your outrage. It's not your enemy. It's your salvation. And remember, 'EVIL IS POWLERLESS IF THE GOOD ARE UNAFRAID.'"

I had had enough of playing it safe both today and in life in general. Enough of this cute humor and spiritual satire. GET REAL, Alan. This dictation today is A SUCICIDE NOTE. Get it all out in the open. Speak your fucking mind or die in regret.

If you're wondering, not even the top psychotherapists in California could figure out how to treat the complex constellation of degenerative brain trauma, excessive meditation dysfunction, celibacy triggered sexual trauma, and inauthentic enlightenment denial. Except, that is, Mr. John Perry, the renowned Jungian Psychiatrist and author of numerous books, including the one that brought me to him, titled: "THE FAR SIDE OF MADNESS."

As it turned out, John and I lived a few houses from each other in Larkspur Canyon, California. I was blessed to visit with him on a regular basis, as he agreed to mentor me in Jungian thought, while fully accepting my "madness as a virtue, not a weakness," as he so often would say. But, unfortunately, John passed on in 1998 and I was bereft of his mentorship.

The only other psychotherapist I trusted was Shakti-Ma, who I also saw regularly for many years, until I moved to Paris. In retrospect, I'm eternally grateful to this blessed woman and felt I should have married her, but she always said, "clients and therapists don't do that kind of thing." And as I recalled her beauty and bravery today, here in the House of Rocky, I felt a deep pang of love for her.

SELF-IMPROVE TO SELF-ANNIHILATE

DESPITE the West's fetish with mindfulness; MINDFUL of every fucking thought of every fucking mindful minute of every fucking low dosing day of mindful Denial, our Doomsday Clock keeps on cranking as if on crack. And now with the people-betraying neoliberals in control of our beloved country while buddied up with the democracy-destroying Chinese Communist Party (C.C.P.), we're standing on the threshold of a frightening new authoritarianism.

As a shrill of fear crept up my spine, my mind quivered in anticipation of a ghastly future with weaponized panic, mass surveillance, lockdowns, mandatory vaccinations, DEPLATFORMING FREE SPEECH, criminalizing human rights, and a BIG BROTHER corporate media where LIES are interchangeable with facts.

TOTALITARISM, INC had begun. And with it, a gloom that will be that much doomier before the clock strikes midnight.

With decades of spiritual activism, engaged Buddhism, and *yoga* off the mat, along with a daily average of 10 billion collective OM's and 100 million mantras, along with the Dalai Lama's international fame by embodying the most celebrated meaning of human decency, NOTHING has stopped GLOBAL GREED, BLIND CONSUMERISM, CORPORATE FACISM, OUR HATRED BOTH OF NATURE and NON-HUMANS, and our INSATIABLE FETISH FOR FOSSIL FUELS.

And now, digital death and perhaps incarceration as well to all those "domestic terrorists" who oppose our decent into militarized fascism, anthropocentric extinction, and those AT THE HELM – the insanely wealthy, morally vacuous oligarchic elite in Silicon Valley, Wall Street, Davos and the White House.

Like drug addicts, billions of us ordinary citizens, along with millions of uber-hip influencers and spiritual gangsters, snort cool and denial through one nostril and blow carbon out through the other. All the while driving hybrids at high speed into Suzuki's brick wall of extinction, hypnotized, as it were, by denial and magical thinking, chanting fetishes, and a NEVER-ENDING QUEST FOR ONENESS.

On a side note, Patrick Moore, co-founder of Green

Peace, called the Green New Deal "completely crazy," just as Derrick Jensen did in his must read (before extinction) book, "Bright Green Lies."

Moore asks the question we're all asking. How the fuck do we grow and transport food for eight billion hungry humans without oil and gas and electricity? How do you get your tofu and granola and face creams to the cities? Horses? Skateboards? On the backs of slave laborers flown in from Tibet?

In paraphrasing his conclusion he states, If fossil fuels were banned today every fucking tree in the world would have to be cut down for the fuel needed for cooking and heating. And that includes the trillion new trees being planted as Alan types. Even if you cut them all down without gas powered chainsaws it's "mass death," sooner than continuing our fossil fuel addiction under the political hack and hypocrite, Joe Biden.

In other words, the "Green New Deal" is nothing other than a barely disguised corporate coup d'état that will result in GLOBAL GENOCIDE. It is yet another dark fairy tale produced by none other than the DEATH WISH cultists in Davos. THEY MUST BE STOPPED.

And let us not forget Greta Thunberg's summary of the crisis today: "In 2010 our leaders signed "ambitious goals to protect wildlife and ecosystems." By TODAY, they'd failed on every single one. Each day they choose not to act. Instead, they sign more "ambitious" non-binding future goals while passing policy locking in destructive business as usual. Bullshit will not save the EARTH, NOR WILL REJOINING THE PARIS AGREEMENT."

As I reflected further, it all felt so perverse: US HUMANS, as it were, willfully killing ourselves and all of nature in order to maintain the lie of normalcy, morality, and the sanctity of life. How strange. But such is cognitive dissonance. Look at how many people smoke knowing that it causes cancer.

SPIRITUAL CAPITAL OF THE UNIVERSE

At the onset of the pandemic I was in Bali, Burma and Byron Bay, three places I've frequented for decades. These hideouts, along with Maui, have been my monasteries, my oases of sanity, homes – places where I have acted out and acted in, discovered myself, fought, loved, and nearly died, numerous times.

Way back, Byron was a quiescent liberated Australian beach town of topless hippies, cool surfers, and some of the first meditators in the Western world. There was so much free sex that some parents had five tiers of children. Almost everyone was a relative. But as condoms caught on, sperm was even recycled into some of the first permaculture farms in the world. One hip scene.

Bali, on the other hand, is fast and loose. As the spiritual capital of the Universe, it's the only place on the planet you can dress year around as if going to a Halloween Party on Atlantis.

It's also a Mecca for Millennial's. And oddly, a place where age matters. Forty and above are dinosaurs. Fifty to sixty, cave dwellers. Sixty and above, almost dead. That is, unless you're a Russian woman, then forty and below are teenagers, and sixty and above, if you have bucks, are liberators, not sugar daddies.

Bali's version of lockdown from Covid is no kissing during orgies, but oral and anal sex allowed. Whereas, for many on the sacred isle, the virus was the long-awaited arrival of the supreme spiritual teacher – the beloved crown jewel *Sri-Corona-gyi*. According to legend, this lethal virus came at this time in human history to teach our species the power of non-separation and that all suffering is merely a mirror for one's lack of devotion to Absolute Unity.

Sadly, folks often criticize the island for its dark underbelly of extortion, drug dealing and generally lawlessness, with bribes for almost everything, even if volunteering to pick up litter or save the lives of dogs and cats. But its redemption is that it's a multi-verse university with awesome classes in "how to live your VERY best life", whether it be a paid influencer, a spiritual gangster, a shadow seer, a bad ass blogger, a new age hooker, a gender fluid *yoga* teacher, a past life medium, a breath worker, a plant medicine merchant, a tarot reader, a conscious crypto trader, a truly authentic leader, or a genuine *tantra* teacher, on and on.

And not surprisingly, Bali is inundated with the most beautiful women in the world. Ironically, they don't come to model or marry, they come to HEAL, and of all things, primarily from sexual trauma. And there is no shortage of slick talking East Indian, Australian and South American men with online degrees in the modern art of *yoni* massage, conscious cunnilingus and rectal penetration toxin removal therapy to help them along their healing journey.

Overall, the place is so fucking rad, you must bring up your children there. Polyamory is mandatory. *Tantra* is taught in tea shops. Commitments are calibrated by the minute. Long term is oral, anal, gone. Bonding is how well the condom fits. Celibacy is a sickness. Kink is what children learn in kindergarten. Non-eye contact is seen as traumatic. Judgment reveals your lack of vulnerability. Criticism is seen as a curse and cause for public stoning. Even upon arrival at the airport you must pledge your obsession for self-improvement and pay $100 bucks or be busted for bringing in Viagra.

I did my show "Spiritually Incorrect" in Ubud at the prestigious Paridiso Theatre, with half the audience standing and shouting and clapping at the end of how much they loved it; another quarter booing, flipping me the finger and yelling "devil"; and the other quarter too stoned to move. Overall, I should have known the neoliberal spiritualized globalists in the theater did not want to hear of their complicity with human generated extinction, especially from a sexually traumatized former Buddhist monk.

I actually had a woman cry when I told her I was both celibate and had refrained from masturbation for the past two years. Another woman concurred that my "non-sexual interest" was the most extreme symptom of sexual trauma she'd ever come across. I wasn't a victim of bypassing, she said, "but enlightened spiritual roadkill."

I did meet one woman who wanted to do mushrooms together, so long as we only snuggle naked. I can't say her name, as she's well known. I thanked her and politely declined saying, "I'm waiting for my twin flame."

She then smiled and threw her arms around me and kissed me. Then gave me her card and walked off saying, "It might be me." That's Bali.

BYRON BAY, LITTLE INDIA

Today, Byron is for the uber wealthy – a magical thinking paradise of Covid carefree movie stars, "real life" influencers, gangster yogis, and hipster families with designer spiritual kids force fed the "Power of Now" and Hindu chanting from birth.

I'm told that that some kids greet teachers with "*Namaste*" and are fluent in Sanskrit by age 12, along with mandatory Broken Ozzie English, of course.

There's a ton of digital nomads lining the beach parks in their shiny bamboo camper vans along with dueling acro *yoga* teachers fiddling their Ukuleles vying for the girls around refillable methane campfires throughout the night.

There's also an elite Mafia class of mega wealthy Israeli drug and arms dealers with hip business fronts to look legit. And there are entire subdivisions in the hinterlands populated with Osho Rajneesh devotees living off their ancient drug money, while clinging to their aging cult of the clit and modernized with full bodied orgasms.

I admit, it was somewhat discombobulating on the one hand, to meet so many intelligent people that were adept at meditation and making intimate eye contact when speaking, and on the other hand, cultivated the "activism of orgasming" as many times in a day as possible as the best way of confronting the climate crisis.

There are even workshops devoted to psychedelic-assisted cumming to confront climate despair. I was given a complimentary pass by an organizer but struggled because I could not get an erection while envisioning dystopia. Oddly, after being caught taking Viagra, I was asked to leave, and told there were no drugs allowed.

On a positive note, there is an inherent ancestral shame that fills the air during most plant medicine ceremonies, as many true Australian participants access the trauma of their white imperialist past and uncover their collusion with the nationwide denial of the genocide of the Indigenous populations. And to their credit, local authorities finally passed legislation to sell locally made didgeridoos and handmade organic cotton ball caps with images of Aboriginal elders in Wollies.

I went to Byron to also perform "Spiritually Incorrect." The show was to be filmed and would form the basis of a feature documentary on my life story. I had agreed to the production as long as it included the good, the true and the most challenging elements of my fifty-year spiritual journey, as well as confronted consumerism, spiritual propaganda and human generated extinction head on.

LOVE IN THE TIME OF EXTINCTION

The day of my show at the Byron Theater, I met a super hip spiritual couple. You see some pretty mean power duos in the hot spots like Canguu, Ko Phangan, Ibiza, and of course, here in Santa Monica too. But these two rocked. Not only did they have that hyper-sexualized chemistry that only true Insta-influencers have, they had that poser gaze of 'look into the camera babe, I want to fuck you every minute of every day, and so does everyone else.' These two were grand masters of pretense and photoshop.

Those of us who know, realize that it takes commitment, practice and emotional intelligence to truly polish and embody your Inner-Imposter. Fraudulence does not come easily, even if you train in it as a monk. It takes time and courage to proudly swag your narcissism in public. We all have the instinct for hypocrisy, but few have the qualities to be paid to post it.

I was shopping at Santos, the hippest organic food store in Australia, and to my surprise, the woman of the couple walked over and with the most angelic voice asked, "Are you Alan Clements?"

Instantly, I knew why I had come to Byron and fell in love on the spot. Not only was she beautiful, but her energy shattered my projection of her, and it took my decades of meditation and courage in working in war zones to maintain my cool.

I said with contrived composure, "Yes." All the while thinking, would you like to go back to my place and meditate together?

She broke my trance, saying, "What an honor to meet you, finally. I mean this, my partner and I drove all the way from Melbourne to see your performance tonight."

Forgetting societal collapse, mass starvation, near-term extinction and the end of Life, for one brief moment, I calmly replied, "I'm honored."

The Angel continued, "I've read your books, "Instinct for Freedom," "The Voice of Hope," and "A Future To Believe In", and they blew my mind."

"Cool," I said. "Really appreciate that you took the time to read them."

Meanwhile, as my mindfulness reasserted its intelligence, I'm thinking 'this woman is marriage material. Do you want to fall in love right here on the spot and have babies and pets and family dinners? I'll even go into therapy to learn how to communicate with someone 35 years younger. I'll even do a neo-tantra workshop with you in Ubud. Anything. I'll even purge with you. Become a certified Reiki teacher, if that's what you want. Anything, please marry me right now. I'm an Officiant, I can do it for us. I'll never speak a word about extinction again.'

She clearly had other things on her mind, and while reaching out her hand to hold mine, she continued, "Let me be totally transparent. I'm not trying to come on to you. But I consulted with a past life regression therapist and she confirmed what I knew deep in my soul."

Yes, I'm thinking with mindful poise. If only she would read my mind. We can do acid together and escape to a safer dimension of the universe. Marry me, now, please.

"The medium told me that you were the love of my life in my last incarnation. And I don't mean a casual affair, Alan. I mean you were my TWIN FLAME. And we were going to get married."

I'm thinking, Jesus, is she channeling me, or is this for real? And if so, let's just pick up where we left off.

She then waves for her boy to come over and introduces him as her fucking partner. I'm sickened with disappointment.

Yoga monkey is about 5' 3" and wearing tight ball contouring *yoga* shorts and is bare chested. He's a miniature Arnold Schwarzenegger and looks at me with his acro *yoga* fake smile and says, "*Namaste*," in a perfectly enunciated 'I did my 200-hour training in Rishekesh' faux-Hindi tone.

Like Joe Biden joking how he would have loved to have punched Trump out if they went to high school together, I felt validated by the President to feel the same with steroid boy.

Fuck your own *Namaste* up your own re-appropriated ass, I thought to myself.

Twerp then reaches out his small spider-like rock-climbing hand as if to shake, and while making unflinching eye contact, I politely smile and break the stare saying, "Please excuse me. I'm not touching others as I hear this Covid thing spreads easily."

Rather, I placed my clasped hands in front of my chest and lowered my head slightly to show honor.

Angel breaks the veil of jealousy and says, "Honey, be mindful of your projections. This is Alan Clements. He's a spiritual savant." Space freezes in contempt.

She continues, "He's the one I keep telling you about. As I've said, I had never been more in love with any human being than Alan. He held me with such grace and an open-hearted non-judgmental space. Never limiting me by his needs or projections.

"You cannot believe how authentic he is and funny too," she continued. "He's truly a fearless human being. Vulnerable. Generous. Caring. Gifted in so many ways. And he cared for me like no other man. He was the best lover I ever had or could imagine having. He came from the heart, not his dick."

Meanwhile, my ego evaporated and I'm aware that I had an erection. It could have been the first since my days as a rock star meditation teacher decades ago.

Yoga boy then says with a slight laugh, "Nice to meet you, sir. If you weren't so old, I'd be jealous. Of course, just joking dude."

"I'm sorry, I missed your name," I asked.

"*Ram*, and this my partner *Mara*."

Ram then says, "I hear you're pretty heavy on the extinction story. I hope you aren't a downer like so many of your generation and project your shit on others."

Could have punched him on the spot. Instead, I buried my integrity and opted for satire, "I hear you. I take most of the blame for the end of life as we know it."

He retorts, "Exactly, you of all people know that you create your own reality."

I'm thinking, you fucking dickhead. Why don't you go back to your tree house and jump over the balcony and do us all a favor as you create your own reality.

But rather than speaking my truth, I politely nod and say, "Yes, you've got a point there. I had always wondered why women enjoyed being gang raped. A spiritual thing, right? Just wanting to evolve their compassion for predators?"

I did the show that night with renewed determination to make the point that extinction would be selective – magical thinking narcissistic male *yoga* teachers would go first. At which point he grabbed Mara's hand and got up and left the show early.

Although she did blow a kiss on the way out, I have never heard from her again. Like *Shakti-Ma*, should have married *Mara* too. Maybe next life, post extinction, we'll all reunite in a new form of marriage, called a long-term sapio-sexual celibate threesome.

I WANT TO KNOW WHAT YOU KNOW

I cannot stop the Doomsday Clock from ticking in my head as I search for hope to face societal collapse. As mindfulness kicks in I'm reminded to just FEEL. Sit back, Alan. Take the future out of time. You are not going to 'think' your way out of conditioned existence. Drop in. Be quiet. Listen. Allow the truth to be revealed, intuitively.

From the silence I see myself at sixteen with a crushed head, returning home from hospital after the car collision with a telephone pole. Magnified by the acid, the trauma of the past felt as if were reoccurring again, NOW. I'm shivering with fear and shame in the House of Rocky, drenched in ancient visions of blood gushing from my skull and screaming at the devil – I'M a MONSTER for LIFE!

I snap back to dinner with my family circa 1966, unable to see from the bandages and the swelling of my eyes firmly shut. The silence is broken when I hear the news on television with Walter Cronkite, telling us, yet again, the numbers of American's killed and injured on this day in Vietnam. I sensed a tension mounting, when my mother gasped. "What's happening?" I asked.

When no one answered, I turned in my chair and pried open an eye to look at the television screen myself. Cronkite was narrating the story of how a Vietnamese Buddhist monk walked to a city square in Saigon, sat crossed legged, doused himself with kerosene, lit a match, and set himself on fire. Apparently, his self-immolation was intended to draw world attention to the victims of America's war; an archetypal sacrifice that symbolized the unjust suffering of his people.

The sickness of the war was one thing, but awe took precedence: I asked myself how was it possible for this monk to sit still while his body burned? The idea was totally alien and at the same time strangely familiar. I just sat there with an eye pried open, transfixed by the miracle and the madness of what I was seeing. The power of that famous image seared itself on my mind.

I went to the washroom to do the unthinkable: face myself. I needed to know what I looked like. I slowly unwound the gauze and I pried open my eye again. I knew it would look bad, but nothing could have prepared me for what I saw in the mirror. I collapsed. Not only was I the ugliest human I'd ever seen, I realized those massive, grotesque scars would remain, a symbol of my stupidity, for life. I was so angry at myself I wanted to die.

But something that night saved me from my darker self. The anger turned to rage, and the rage carried with it the sheer force of determination. I flashed on an image of that burning Buddhist monk. I saw him reflected in the mirror. How could I transcend my body? How could I transcend pain? What inner reserves did he draw on in choosing a noble death?

I entered the projection of his burning body and pledged, "I want to know what you know." I remembered, yet again, that this was the driving metaphor that fueled my idea of the spiritual journey, of facing whatever, come what may, and burn for the truth if needed. I then heard Bob coming through me; "NEVER GIVE UP, Alan. The fight is just beginning."

NOTRE DAME CATHEDRAL

Back in the House of Rocky, I imagined Bob's study – lined with hundreds of books floor to ceiling, ancient Buddha statues, a grand piano, fine paintings, a large Tibetan Tanka, and colorful Tiffany lamps – to be Notre Dame. I could see the Cathedral's radiant holy nature come alive within the hallucination of my inner *Mandala*, as if her medieval magnificence were 4-D real.

I had lived in Paris in the mid-90's and find myself back there again, in my mind's eye, on the day that I learned that my dear friend, Win Htein, a Burmese freedom fighter, was arrested, interrogated and tortured for 28 days, before being thrown into BIG BROTHER'S gulag to rot in TOTALITARIAN HELL with a broken body.

For months Win Htein had arranged for my secretive meetings with Aung San Suu Kyi that led to our book of conversations, "The Voice of Hope." Once the THOUGHT POLICE learned of our endeavor I was thrown out of the country, vilified in the State media as public enemy #1, and permanently banned from reentering Burma for the next 17 years, until unexpectedly pardoned by the President.

A year before Paris, I was living in the former Yugoslavia during their war that turned my life inside out. Now, memories began to resurface of being in candle-lit underground nightclubs, drinking, doing ecstasy and smoking, and talking with friends about love, existentialism, demonization, and the politics of genocide.

Seeing firsthand humankind's EVIL urge to annihilate its own species in the name of God, ideology, nationality, religion, POWER, MONEY, PRIVLEDGE, and any number of other perversities masquerading as TRUTH & FREEDOM, sicked me.

And today, in House of Rocky, I heard Win Htein's torturous SCREAMS and became FRIGHTENED and nauseous. Struggling to keep from heaving, I reached for the morphine to end this Orwellian NIGHTMARE. Too weak to inject the syringe, I collapsed into the thickening darkness and lay on the carpet, knowing it was only going to get worse, as the flashbacks became more real.

After the WAR I moved from Zagreb to Sarajevo to continue writing the film that Bob had commissioned on the meaning of 'LOVE IN THE TIME OF GENOCIDE.' And today, in a life and death acid trip in his very house, the theme took on even greater significance, viewed through the lens of human driven extinction.

I'm driving with my old friend along a narrow, broken road in the war-torn countryside of rural Bosnia. We've just left the ghost town of Srebrenica, where several thousand Muslim men and boys were separated from the women and systematically slaughtered one by one by Bosnian Serb paramilitary forces. And the women and girls raped and "ethnically cleansed" as they tried to flee.

After hours driving through bombed-out villages, we stopped by the side of the road to take a break. In a nearby field some men were digging. We walked over and found a mass grave — a pit of putrefying human flesh. It was heart-wrenching and frightening. We gasped from the stench.

But this wasn't anything new, I reflected. The human world is fraught with murderous expressions of ethnocentricity, xenophobia, and nationalism. The twentieth century has been witness to obscene brutality. Stalin. The Holocaust. Hiroshima. The genocides in Timor, Rwanda and Tibet. The Apocalypse in Syria. Pinochet's terror in Chile. Pol Pot's sea of cracked skulls in Cambodia. The death squads of Guatemala. Saddam Hussein's massacre of the Kurds. The crushing of democracy in Burma and Tiananmen Square. The hanging of Ken Saro-Wiwa in Nigeria. In the name of what? Truth? Freedom? Nationalism? Globalization? Christ? Allah? Oil? God? Money?

I came back briefly to the present to stabilize and then closed my eyes again to focus on the mass grave. Protruding from the ground, I saw an exposed hand with a ring on one of the fingers, glistening in the sunlight. I stared at the ring for a long time. There was no way of telling whether it was a man or woman, but the ring spoke to me today of the broken bond of human decency and the OUTRAGE I felt for the inherent cruelty of life.

Back inside Notre Dame, yet again I hear Win Htein's tortured screams. I drop to my knees to pray and cry and RAGE at this fucking INSANE universe, screaming out in my pain – you FUCKING ASSHOLE GOD! Fuck this sick creation. It's a BAD DESIGN! One rape is too many. One Holocaust is too many. One extinction is too many. I want OUT!

Suddenly, the voice of an imaginary Buddha softened my rage, stating: "Alan, from an inconceivable beginning you have been born and transmigrated, life after life. A beginning point to this *Samsara* is not evident; though hindered by ignorance and fettered by craving, you are thus transmigrating and wandering on and on and on, life after life.

"I tell you, Alan. Far greater than all the water in the four great oceans is the blood you have shed from being slaughtered while transmigrating and wandering this long, long time in *Samsara*. And the same, Alan, crying for those near and dear to you who have been killed – you have shed more tears than the water in the four great oceans.

"Turn away, Alan, or soon you too will meet this fate, yet again. Walk out of this house of HORROR."

I called out for Bob but his words of encouragement were not to be found. I was burning alone in the mirror of my own immolation, in the House of Rocky that suddenly froze over with RADICAL self-doubt.

I reached out again for the morphine, but the acid was so strong it took everything to steady a wobbling hand and the syringe. I had never been so close to injecting it and kept trying and even pricked my skin and it began to bleed.

As I watched the blood run down my arm I imagined how long and how many lifetimes it would take to fill the oceans, and how many extinctions would come and go, and earths and solar systems as well.

For the next while I cried, and as I watched the tears mix with blood, oddly, there was a strange sense of relief in knowing how easily I could end my life. And for a BRIEF moment, it allowed me some level of acceptance of the Apocalypse that was soon to come.

I laid back down on the carpet and closed my eyes and continued to cry. It was all an inner game at this point, an existential *Mandala* of intersecting symbols within my own Wheel of Life and my own personal War with *Samsara*. I cried and cried, until I forgot why, but knew somewhere trustful and deep that the fight was just beginning.

GRETA AT THE UN

Greta Thunberg, the Swedish eco-activist, is coming through as she addresses the 193 representatives of the United Nations, WARNING: our precious planet is soon to be uninhabitable from overheating due to our addiction to fossil fuels, consumerism, and a sociopathic disregard for nature and non-humans.

I see her in my mind's eye as vividly as the Vietnamese monk immolating himself on the world's stage fifty-five years before. Greta's presence is equally on fire, as she states: "You have stolen my dreams and my childhood with your empty words. People are suffering. People are dying. ENTIRE ECOSYSTEMS ARE COLLAPSING. WE ARE IN A MASS EXTINCTION, and all you can talk about is money and fairy tales of eternal economic growth."

What would it take for the world to hear, I wondered? Would any of us live differently if Greta immolated herself live on TV from the UN? Does anyone really change, voluntarily, unless they're at rock bottom – on the street and near death – with a needle of whatever dangling from their arm?

I'm imagining millions of years from now – post extinction, eons after the last Wisdom 2.0 Conference on Mindful Stress Reduction After Being Deplatformed from Social Media. A UFO has landed on a dystopian Southern California landscape. We see faux-flesh covered human-like robotic figures walking down a holographic ramp of light, operated by an Artificial Intelligence ten million years more advanced than our own.

After stepping onto the nature-barren landscape and taking a few selfies and group shots, the AI-entities stop scrolling their Facebook accounts after being ordered from Headquarters to do an archaeological Google search for "what the fuck happened to this civilization?"

Uninspired, the AI-captain forces himself away from his Head Space App and presses 'X-ray vision one mile deep' on his light-generated iPhone. Instantly we see in his computer chip perfected 4-D mind, a cinematic vision of a network of fossilized automobiles, with petrified entities in them. As the AI-aliens scan the underground horizon, we visually travel along a vast network of petrified S.U.V's, trucks, and buses, bummer to bummer for hundreds of miles.

The captain presses "access landscape – dialectical deduction" and a BOLD caption reads, 'looks like yet another fossil fuel driven globalist civilization got carried away with their BANKRUPT DEMOCRACY, consumerism, and CASH-IS-GOD GREED.'

"Oh well, let's bolt guys," the captain says, "and return home in our Tesla light stream beam. And let's bring some of those masks covering their faces. They might give us a clue to their cult leader."

If meditation taught me anything, it was to look no further than myself for answers. If there was to be extinction, and there will be sooner or later, I asked, how is it that I too am participating in the mass murder of life? And equally, what can I do to prepare for the collapse?

It was not until I read a recent interview with Greta in the "New York – once upon a – Times", titled, "Greta Hears Your Gibberish and Is Unimpressed," that I began to understand more clearly my own blind spots and the epic challenge of finding solutions to the greatest existential crisis humankind has ever faced.

Beyond Greta making the point that our earthly house was STILL ON FIRE with our ADDICTION to DENIAL, I was struck by her matter of fact communication skills.

How direct and uncompromising she was and unwilling to be glorified, even dismissive of compliments, saying: "I don't give a shit whether others see me as a child or an adult, nor do I give a damn what others think of me. I'm not going to dumb-down to fit the needs of others."

She went onto say, "People often say to me: She's trying to frame herself as a child so that people can't criticize her. She's using that as a shield."

To this Greta replies, "That's dead wrong, ass wipe. I'm autistic. That means I'm without ego. And I say things the way they are. I'm not trying to court favor and applause or impress others like brainwashed meat puppets do. Frankly, I couldn't give a rat's ass what others think of me. Again, that's because I'm autistic, dingbat. And I have Asperger's as well. So if you don't mind, buzz off, air head."

I'm thinking this girl is speaking my language, literally. Had she been channeling me, I wondered?

Beyond the GRIM message of societal collapse and near-term human extinction, Greta's bold ass use of language inspired me. Then, it came like a bolt of lightning, how fucking safe I play it. Compared to this courageous young woman, you're a crevice-dwelling weak-kneed mumble mouth, Alan.

And further, you've denied a fundamental part of your own personality structure: You do not OWN your autistic inner child. Nor do you OWN your Asperger's.

Nor do you OWN your fucking Tourette's syndrome –Yes, that's right. You're down with your traumatic brain injury but that does not account for your insatiable appetite for fucking expletives. Get it, Alan, you have advanced Tourette's – that's right – a neurological disorder characterized by the compulsive use of fucking obscenities.

Face it, Alan, mindfully. You have autism, Asperger's, Advanced Tourette's Syndrome, Inauthentic Enlightenment Dysfunction, Excessive Meditation Disorder, Chronic Brain Trauma, Celibacy Induced Sexual Trauma, an eating disorder, and you are a "long hauler" with permanent Covid complications. And there's the strong likelihood of narcissism and bipolar as well, and probably much more due to your pathological level of denial and self-deception. Remember dude, you thought you were Enlightened. That in itself makes you a nutter.

It all started to make sense. No wonder you don't like people, Alan. And that's precisely why people struggle with you. Get it, you're a psychological catastrophe. Damaged goods. And of course, that's also your mad genius and precisely why Sayadaw U Pandita, Bob, Shakti-Ma and John Perry loved you so much.

That's IT – I GOT IT! Alan, you simply don't give a shit what the fuck others think of you. No wonder you resonate with Donald Trump and Steven Bannon and Howard Stern and Bill Maher and Ricky Gervais and Bill Hicks. They're Brothers of dysfunction. And they're also MAD geniuses, precisely because they ACT with

CONFIDENCE AND SPEAK THIER MIND, despite being seriously flawed.

And that's why you struggle with Biden – as much as you try to like him, he comes across as phony, without credibility, an arrogant moron dead-eyed machine politician programmed on vaseline and profit, who pontificates about moral courage and conscious politics, but refuses to embody those very principles. What you see is not what you get. I wish it wasn't so, but HE FOLLOWS THE MONEY and is a sell-out hiding behind $20,000 of face-work. And the same with most politicians and sadly, spiritual teachers too.

This was the GREAT Awakening I had always been waiting for. It was nothing less than the Enlightenment of Trauma – a radical self-compassion for one's imperfection.

Everything was falling into place. No wonder I cannot make clear decisions at the day-to-day crossroads of my life. No wonder I OCD-ed on mindfulness. No wonder all those years of psychotherapy ended with the start of decades of anti-depressants. The list of odd behaviors, compulsions and emotional quirks kept making more and more sense, as if the puzzle of my life was finally beginning to assemble into a fractured whole.

Quite frankly, reading this acid-illuminated interview with sister Greta was having much more of a transformational impact on me than reading both "Be Here Now" and "Practical Insight Meditation Instructions" did fifty years before, and on acid, no less.

I kept reading as the interviewer continued his assault on dear Greta saying, "I understand that it's ridiculous to ask an arrogant teen about complicated geopolitical problems, but you're not ten anymore and you're a world leader now. Is there an age at which you would consider it reasonable for people to expect that you start having real ideas about real solutions to save humanity from killing itself?"

"Are you for real, bonehead?" she replies. "Real ideas? Real solutions? What, go to an ashram? Change your lame ass Christian name to a Hindu deity? Do a chanting workshop with Krishna Dass? Buy a mala with Eckhart Tolle's mug on it? Get a few tattoos? Purge my childhood trauma? Get out of my face, dough brain, or I may change my mind about extinction and pray it happens sooner, and only for you."

How is it, I thought, I can think and write these things, but can't say them in real life? Why the gap? It has to be because I've not yet embraced my mentally challenged true nature. Get it, Alan, you've been pretending to be mindful for five decades and now you're finally becoming aware of yourself AS YOU REALLY ARE. You not only bypassed your essential personality structure, you tunneled under your true self and have been living as a mindfully damaged cave dweller.

Greta breaks me from my psychedelic-assisted self-therapy and responds to the interviewer, saying: "I read and study the climate crisis we're in, but frankly I'm no expert on human generated mass murder. I know much more about communicating and language than I do about the death of our oceans, the genocide of non-humans, the melting of the polar caps, methane bombs, sea level rise, coastal degeneration, and the escalating Anthropocentric annihilation of ALL LIFE, as we know it.

"See, when speaking with corporate media propagandists like you, one always had to be upbeat and positive, otherwise you wouldn't print it. For me, I communicate reality, and further, just because everyone is doing something doesn't make it right.

"To change, we need to understand that we are headed towards DARKNESS with no running water, no electricity, and no New York Times, along with mass starvation and dystopian violence. In other words, your Twitter and Facebook feeds will soon be meaningless, especially when cannibalism becomes the norm. Read Cormac McCarthy's book, "The Road," to get a dose of reality.

"Get it! We cannot pretend anymore and offer up false hope. It's morally wrong. So I communicate the climate emergency as it is. Which means with clarity and straight talk. Call me the Donald Trump of eco-activism, if you like. But such threats mean nothing to me. Donald and I may not see eye to eye, but I'm confident that he will come around sooner or later, especially once he's humbled.

"So, if you don't mind, please get out of my face,

knucklehead, or I'll have you impeached. Just joking. It's America's dysfunctional influence on me."

And the reporter responds: "Wow. Never expected that. But thank you for your frankness, Greta. Another question, if I may: In the past you've attributed your clarity not on your practice of mindfulness, but due to your Asperger's syndrome — you've even called it your 'superpower.' If I may, "Are there any ways in which Asperger's has set you back and is a hindrance?"

Greta responds, saying, "What? You're an unrelenting fart knocker. Am I handicapped by Asperger's, asshole? Could be, if you think having a sell-out normal life is better. I mean, you work for the Times and as I said, it's a propaganda machine for the neoliberal totalitarian globalists. You work there because you went to Harvard and you probably think you're better than I am. If you think that, screw you.

"Now, did I say that because of autism or Asperger's? Who gives a shit, right? The fact is, it's true. And if you're wondering, I don't dislike you. I just think you are a brain-dead propaganda-spouting puppet of the left with a huge insecurity problem, very much like Donald Trump and Joe Biden as well, for that matter."

Greta concludes by saying, "People with Asperger's and autism like Alan and I, and millions of others too, don't follow social codes, if you haven't noticed. As we both said, we don't give a damn what people think about us. That's why we started to act for the future of life, and I strongly believe it's why people on the autism spectrum, like us, are the ONLY ones truly making a difference in attempting to stop the Doomsday Clock and possibly prevent an Apocalypse."

Suddenly, my higher self was interrupted by the calm clear voice of my psychiatrist from our Zoom session earlier in the day. "Alan, if you choose to record yourself before you take your life, make the point that everything transcribed is self-generated and not real life. Extinction is real, of course. But everything one may hear and or read are symbols in your own inner process. They are about you, not others.

"Also, it is my professional opinion that much of what you are dealing with is ecological grief from the anticipation of anthropocentric horror. And I may add, this is exacerbating your deteriorating cognitive skills from your traumatic brain injury as a teenager and subsequent years of head traumas and concussions as a wide receiver at UVA.

"As we've discussed, your memory loss, suicidal ideation, dizziness, and overall disorientation, may well be symptoms of CTE – chronic traumatic encephalopathy – and also early-to-mid-stage dementia.

"I know you wanted to be tested but I checked into it and MRI's are ineffective in discovering CTE. I know you haven't told anyone about your condition. And it really saddens me to think that you were a wide receiver for all those years after your accident. It's tragic no one knew at that time that playing football alone was enough to cause early death. But you've been a long-term meditator, so let's hope for the best.

"Alan, I'll see you next Wednesday at 2 pm for our next session. I'll send you the link early next week. And please don't forget to take your meds. As you know, you've been in lockdown for months and isolated, and a long hauler, along with these recurring thoughts of taking your own life... Well, I'm really concerned. You have my number, and you must assure me that you will call me anytime 24/7. Okay?"

THE MAGIC CHRISTIAN

Jump time, to the "Magic Christian," a satirical comedy exposing the dark underbelly of corporate capitalism, starring Peter Sellers, Ringo Starr, and John Cleese – long before Monty Python formed. The premise of the film is that 'everyone has a price', regardless of one's conscience, morals or political beliefs.

In an early scene, we see a policeman joyously eating a traffic ticket he issued to Peter Sellers, for a mere few hundred bucks. In another scene, we see a famous Shakespearean actor at a packed London theater breaking script as Hamlet and begin stripping, eventually swirling his shlong in the face of a British Royal in a front row seat, both embarrassed and turned on, at the same time. There's another scene of a televised group of sophisticated British hunters stalking pheasants in an open field, when suddenly the star huntsman is driven in, manning an anti-aircraft gun mounted on a jeep, and obliterates a single bird as it attempts to fly away. All willingly done, of course, for a price.

The film ends with Peter and Ringo erecting a large outdoor vat in the financial district of downtown London. We see a large container truck arrive and a man gets out and pumps the vat full of animal urine, blood and excrement. On the side of the vat Ringo paints a BOLD RED sign that reads, FREE MONEY.

Slowly, men in fancy black suits approach the vat, while covering their noses to block the stench. Once at the vat, the men are seen cautiously dipping their hands into the vat to pluck out big bills, one by one.

Eventually, EXTREME GREED gets the better of the global capitalists and they step down into the vat of waist deep liquefied animal entrails, until they say, one by one, "fuck it," and submerge fully – head and all – under the surface of the liquefied shit. ALL FOR MONEY, of course.

AN ENCOUNTER AT CHECKOUT

"The Magic Christian" got me thinking. I recalled shopping for groceries in preparation for my journey today. I went to Pavillions on Montana, a few blocks away, here in

Santa Monica. I was standing in the express line masked up with a bottle of Japanese Scotch, an avocado, a tomato, some cheese, and a pint of chocolate Haagen-Dazs. My first or last super, I wasn't sure.

In front of me in the express line was a masculine millennial in a blue suit, wearing leather shoes, with wireless ear buds, scrolling his social media feed with one hand and rubbing his Jack Dorsey-like beard with the other.

His highly polished spiritual prick demeanor was amplified by his flagrant violation of express checkout rules: he had no items. Worse, he was now talking to a broker about buying stock options in Moderna, saying, "It doesn't matter that I don't trust the vaccine. I want in before it skyrockets."

Compartmentalizing my judgment with a high degree of mindful intelligence, I wondered why the fuck such a bonehead would be in the express line without any items, while holding up the rest of us.

As we stood there, I mindfully reeled in my prayer for his economic ruin and sent him waves of contempt-filled loving kindness that made my psyche quiver with repressed joy. All those years of ardent meditation were clearly paying off.

To my surprise, he stopped the conversation with his broker and asked the female checkout clerk for a pack of Marlboro Lights. Instantly my judgment turned into genuine compassion for the asshole: he's a smoker.

As my empathy evolved, I reflected on how stressful his life must be to be addicted to tobacco. I knew the horrors of nicotine all too well. It took thirty years of smoking to finally retire one of the best runs of my life, but only after watching two aunts suffocate with emphysema.

The clerk came back from the cigarette cabinet and handed him a pack of Lights with the warning label image face up: We see a man with his chest cut wide open exposing two blackened splayed lungs with several golf ball sized tumors on them. The caption reads: "SMOKING KILLS. This Is You If You Keep Smoking."

The millennial nodded his head to indicate, No, I don't want this one. And politely said, "Another pack, please. I'm too sensitive for this type of image and it could trigger latent trauma." And he went right back into his conversation with his broker about buying stock options in Moderna.

The clerk returned with another pack and handed him one with a photograph of an middle-age white man with a tracheotomy and a plastic tube coming out of the large hole in his throat to allow him to breath. I looked in close and the caption read: "SMOKING IS LETHAL. Stop Now Or This Will Be You."

The millennial shook his head NO again and calmly said to the clerk, "This one would inhibit my *yoga* practice. Plus, I do *pranayama* to prevent this from happening. Save that for someone who is unskilled in self-care.

Another one please."

She then asked, "What the fuck one do you want, dude?"

He then said to the person he was speaking with on the phone, "Love, please wait a second," and told the clerk, "I'm sorry this triggered you. If you don't mind, I'll have the one with the deformed fetus, please."

As I shook my head in disbelief, I inhaled more deeply the Buddha's injunction that we humans are like children playing in a house on fire – oblivious to the smell of fairy tales and our role in the sixth mass extinction.

I then heard Bob interrupt my reflection, saying, "Alan, stay with it. You're getting closer to the answer. Up your game a bit."

OM AT THE PUMP

I imagined putting WARNING LABELS on all things harmful. Little things to start, like petrol stations. We all know that every gallon kills. But fuck it, we say. It's a necessary evil we're forced to use, so we eat our conscience, suck our humility and dive into the vat of S.H.I.T. And keep on buying this life-annihilating poison to transport ourselves to soul-sucking jobs, in order to repress the stress, and embody the spiritual paralysis of a lifelong depression. A small price to pay to eat, sleep and repeat the lie to die, and kill everyone else as well in the process.

But the world is evolving. Corporations are waking

up. Like BIG tobacco and heavy taxes, BIG Oil will soon initiate a "Go Green or Die" public safety campaign, with announcements on 'the lethality of using their products.' And in so doing, show how they too are doing their part in slowing the march towards extinction.

I'm imagining displays with large Earth-like plastic spheres on large poles entering gas stations; each burning, as it were, with brightly lit neon red and yellow faux flames and under each plastic Earth in bold print: "OIL KILLS CHILDREN, and you too."

Once you drive up to the pump, after inserting your credit card, in a deal between Big Oil and Big Tech, everything is known about you through AAI – a personalized tracking system coordinated with mandatory vaccinations and micro-chips in one's head, known as Omnipotent Mindfulness, or "OM," for short.

What is Advanced Artificial Intelligence? "AAI" are systems that combine the most sophisticated hardware and software on Earth with elaborate databases and knowledge-based processing models based on not-so-secretly stealing every aspect of every second of Facebook's 2.7 billion active users (and that of Gab, Signal, Telegram, Instagram and Twitter too) to demonstrate characteristics infinitely more effective than human decision making.

The OM app, designed by those loyal to Elon Musk along with a rogue set of Silicon Valley *yoga* and tech AAI engineers, is based on the Edward Snowden Algorithm, and is aptly referred to within the eco-activist cancel-the-CANCEL culture community as the Big Brother Protection of Privacy Protocol.

Every time you use your C.C.P. Global One Card, everything is known about you. What does OM know? Think of your personal data as the digital record of everything you know and do both online and in the world. Such as how many swipes to wipe your butt, what paper you used and how many squares, and when and at what time you dental flossed, your calorie intact, the day-to-day evaluation of your integrity, if you lied and to whom and why; everything; even counts the number of NOWS you were present in the day, and the quality of your mindfulness on a scale of 1 to 1000.

Of course, all the most obvious things are registered; every search, purchase, like, swipe, emoticon, text, email, and phone call is recorded. Everything you have ever thought and done, along with every masturbatory fantasy and memory and dream is artificially analyzed and integrated into the OM blockchain. And it includes all Zoom sessions with your psychotherapist as well. OM is, in fact, a much more factual and reliable version of yourself, than you.

And with each gallon pumped, a Siri-like voice meant specifically for you begins to talk. Greetings, Alan, nice to have you back, life killer. Need a bit of gas, Mr. Mindfulness Activist Fraudster? How's your Covid treating you today?

Grateful for my monastic training and fifty years of discernment, I tune out OM and keep mindfully pumping, while practicing *yoga* off the mat – embodied presence – feeling the physical sensations in my body and aware of both the pressure and coolness in my hand as I squeeze the nozzle tightly.

As I approach three gallons, the pumping automatically slows like a poor internet connection circa 1998, and Siri says, "Alan, you of all people, Mr. former Buddhist monk, sexually autistic satirist, blah blah blah, with a litany of flimsy exaggerated probably faked credentials – in fact, we've fact checked your sorry ass – and here you go again, killing off the future of life, just to get laid? Hey, horny loser. Give it up, old guy. Put the fucking pump back in the holder and be on your way!"

At four gallons OM states: "You best stop here, asshole, or we'll consider restricting your Facebook, Instagram and Twitter accounts." I pause, but go, fuck it. It's just AAI, it ain't that real and I hate the Oligarchs of Silicon Valley anyway. And thank OM for helping me break my addiction.

I carry on and double down – mindfully tuning OM out as I did dogs barking in the monastery – and keep pumping. As I hit six gallons, I've been pumping for thirty minutes and OM says, "Persistent fucker you are. You lose, all your social media accounts are done for a month. Way to go prick. Keep it up and you'll be deplatformed. Think of how that is going to play out for your online course and live-streaming. And if you don't instantly hang the fucking pump up, asswipe, we are going to label you a DOMESTIC TERRORIST and turn you into the FBI."

I lose it and shout back, "Fuck you, OM! I'm not afraid of your taunts and threats."

OM shouts back, "You'll regret it, Mr. Mindfulness. You know we have connections in the White House."

"And I know Steven K. Bannon," I SHOUT BACK. "And if you have done your research dimwit, you'll also know that I work for the CIA, so FUCK YOU."

"Playing hard ball, okay. You win," OM says in a tone of resignation. Then asks in a sweet seductive voice, "How about some pussy tonight?"

I reply, "You creep." I look right into the pump's faceless feckless COMMUNIST face and say, "Don't speak with me in such a denigrating way. Pussy is called *yoni* and if you haven't learned *Sanskrit* yet, refer to it as a sacred garden. Nor am I looking for a one-night stand."

OM responds, "Why so triggered, smart guy? Anyway, in that case, don't you think it's high time we introduced you to your Twin Flame? And you know we know exactly who she is and where she is."

I paused and stopped pumping and say, "Okay, now we're talking, OM. You've never laid this one on me before. What do you know?"

"No problem, dude," OM replies. "I've got your back covered. Just hang up the pump and pay your bill with "Eye Pay" and leave a $100 tip. And remember "Iris Guard" has its eyes on you 24/7 and we'll blind you for a month and even take some of your Bitcoin if you contest the charge. And be proud, Alan, you're only a loser foot solider of genocide and not a global leader of mass extinction."

INDEPENDENCE DAY

I relaxed and mindfully noticed the sensations rippling through my body – an anatomical flow of high energy waves along a landscape of ancient emotions, punctuated only by the beat of my heart.

I focused more fully, feeling a timelessness within each pulse, and yet, with each beat a reminder of mortality and a Clock that just keeps on ticking.

I opened the awareness to include the kaleidoscopic swirl of symbolic images and patterns of information within my self-generated *Mandala* – my Wheel of Life and my OWN War with *Samsara*. And this ONGOING existential struggle of perpetual choices with endless crossroads, forced upon us, whether we like it or not.

I look more mindfully into a set of historic images hoping to extract new meaning in the present. As I do, I'm simultaneously transported back to Burma, January 4, 1996, and into the future, and back again to a transient Earth.

I'm at Aung San Suu Kyi's home in Rangoon, a place I've come to know through months of secretive conversations with her and other revolutionaries in their struggle for freedom. I hear the sounds of jubilation in the festive air. As a Westerner dressed in Burmese attire, I'm unrecognizable as I mingle among several hundred of the country's most prominent democracy activists.

They're celebrating Independence Day – in defiance of dictatorship, with gatherings of five or more a crime against the State, and punishable by imprisonment, torture, even death by starvation or rape.

The revolutionary atmosphere was alive with traditional theater, music, singing, storytelling, puppetry and classical dance. And radiant with the peoples' love of harmlessness as the most effective means to fight totalitarian tyranny.

I took a moment to let history transport her magic through the existential arteries of the past to EMBOLDEN MY TRUTH TODAY. Remember "WHY" you are here, Alan. To decide whether life is worth living; everything else is irrelevant.

On the lake side of Aung San Suu Kyi's compound, the curtain opened on the makeshift stage. And to the joy of all gathered, Par Lay, the country's preeminent spoken word satirist, appeared.

Many say that the seeds of Orwell's totalitarian classic "1984" was birthed during his years in Burma as a policeman. And my translator explained, Par Lay's performances brought new meaning to BIG BROTHER, so much so that telling the truth was not only a revolutionary act, but one met with prison, torture and often death.

As Par Lay took the mic, I was told that he had just been released the day before from a hard labor camp in the north. His CRIME: satirizing Burma's military dictator at his last gig. And this was Par Lay's first act upon release, traveling underground from Mandalay to perform here on Independence Day – the very day fifty years before that Burma unchained herself from 135 years of British Imperialism.

Par Lay continued, "For six years I've been pounding rocks, twenty hours a day, with leg and arm irons on, waiting for this moment to perform again."

I tried to imagine his reality: Chained at a crossroads for six years pounding rocks, without a choice of which road to take. Both forks pointed back to where he was standing, pounding rocks. And I heard his totalitarian master shouting in my head, "Put your head down. Pound those rocks. Do as I say! Do not dare think of tomorrow or even today. Lift that pickax and keep pounding. And never forget, you're a criminal and our slave."

Par Lay continues, "Let me offer a few reminders from our brother George Orwell. Although he lived with us back in the 40's, his spirit lives on today. He said, "A people that would allow themselves to be dominated by corrupt generals, politicians, impostors, thieves and traitors – as they do not only here in Burma, but all over the world, especially in China, Russia, and North Korea – are not victims, but accomplices.

"Although counter-intuitive," he explained, "the greater the understanding of the beast, the greater the delusion; the more intelligent the true human, the less sane. Therefore, feel that staying human is essential, even when it feels like it can't have any result, and in so doing, you've beaten them. And if liberty means anything, it means the right to tell impostors what they do not want to hear, especially if they refer to themselves as a military general.

"With that said, I know that today's show will land me be back in prison. But so be it. FREEDOM IS MORE IMPORTANT THAN FEAR."

For the next two hours Par Lay and his Moustache Brothers dazzled the audience with biting satire aimed squarely at the evil of the military dictatorship in his own country, and the totalitarian meme embedded in the mind of most every "democratically elected freedom-loving leader," worldwide.

People laughed and cried and got up and danced in a revolutionary expression of MORAL REBELLION; a virtue I drew from here in the House of Rocky, to further fuel my escalating War with Fear and Terminal Resignation.

And sure enough, the day after his show, Par Lay was

picked up in the middle of night by the TOTALITARIAN MILITARY POLICE and carted off without trail and sentenced to six more years in a hard labor camp pounding rocks, with arm and leg irons, twenty hours a day.

"Alan, Bob here. GO FOR IT."

A CLOCKWORK ORANGE

An epiphany: I entered "A Clockwork Orange," Stanley Kubrick's cinematic masterpiece in societal brainwashing and its purging through radical conversion therapy.

In it, Malcolm McDowell, the protagonist, plays Alex – a charismatic, antisocial deviant, whose passions include classical music, serial rape, and a range of other forms of "ultra-violence," as they're called in the film.

Alex is a morally rotten sexual-psycho, who symbolizes the predator patriarchy of "forever wars and oligarchic-globalism" and inflicts wickedness with a psychotic demeanor of pathological disassociation and sociopathic delight.

After a few years into his prison sentence, Alex eagerly takes up an offer to be a test subject for the Minister of the Interior's new soul cleansing technique; an experimental compassion-based aversion therapy for rehabilitating male psychos within days.

We see Alex strapped to his chair, eyes clamped wide open. He's injected with a drug. Then forced to watch torture porn, accompanied by the inspiring music of his favorite composer, Ludwig van Beethoven.

When Alex gets an erection while watching rape, he simultaneously becomes nauseated by the sexual violence he's forced to watch, and, fearing that the conversion therapy will make him permanently sick upon hearing his beloved Beethoven, he BEGS the Authorities for an end to the healing treatment.

But no such luck. Alex remains belted to the "anti-indoctrination chair" with his eyes clamped wide open while continually force-fed torture and rape porn, sound tracked by his cherished Ludwig.

Days later, at the end of his conversion-therapy, the Minister demonstrates the effectiveness of Alex's rehabilitation to a gathering of officials. We see Alex become sick from wanting to have sex with a stripper.

The prison's spiritual counselor is furious and complains that Alex has been brainwashed and robbed of his mindfulness and free will. But the Minister asserts that the technique will cut crime, alleviate overcrowding in prisons, and moreover, be made into an innovative mindfulness-based anti-indoctrination conversion app. Thus, bringing in much needed revenue while providing a higher degree of professionality to counter the stress of prison officials having to work with the more hardcore terrorists and Jihadists infiltrating the EU from Africa and the Middle East.

We then see Alex leaving his prison retreat a free man and is even presented with a course completion diploma.

Back in the House of Rocky, I'm thinking, how can the wisdom gained from The Magic Christian, LSD, Srebrenica, Par Lay and A Clockwork Orange stop the DOOMSDAY CLOCK and save the world from human generated extinction?

DRAWING UPON THE PSYCHIC INTUITIVE

I hear Bob: "Do whatever is necessary, Alan, to help save America from darkness, and the world too. All it takes is a meta-meme that goes viral. Just as "Rocky" did: You hear the word and we instantly feel: FIGHT ON, NEVER GIVE UP!"

Drop in, I encouraged myself. Today is the most important day of your life. Let TRUTH be revealed. Embody your finest, Alan. Tap into your psychic-intuitive skills to see the past and future, simultaneously. Look. See. Feel. Know. And ACT.

After reflecting on my respect for Bob, Thomas Jefferson, the *Buddha*, *Dhamma* and *Sangha*, and recommitting myself to the future of LIFE, I called for a MORE URGENT sense of mindfully AWAKENED PATRIOTISM. And as I did, the LIGHT of a new dawn PRISMED through the acid. Low and behold, from within the rainbow an orange tinted hallow emerged surrounding a 4-D image of America's Greatest President, Donald J. Trump.

At first, I was startled – as in WTF? – until my mindfulness reasserted itself and intercepted the reaction.

Thus, allowing the radiant stature of America's 45th President to shine brightly, illuminating the interior of the House of Rocky.

"Who are you to me, Sir?" I asked with high *dharma* purpose.

"I am the VENGEFUL warrior archetype within your self-generated *MANDALA*, your Own Inner Wheel of Life," came the President's response. "And like a Star War's force for CONFRONTING EVIL, I am the ONLY WAY you can Win Your War With *Samsara* and put an end to your own S.H.I.T., once and for all."

"HOLY SHIT," I shouted. What an unexpected turn of events. "Speak with me, Sir, please. What is it that I should know?"

The President's distinctive voice channeled through me stating: "Alan, as President of the United States of America and the greatest democracy the world has ever known, I have no higher duty than to defend the laws and the Constitution of our great Republic.

"That is why I am determined to protect our election system, which is now under coordinated assault by the Wall Street-driven, C.C.P. supplicating Democrats. There have been shocking irregularities, abuses and massive fraud, especially evident in the key swing states of Arizona, Georgia, Michigan, Nevada, Pennsylvania, and Wisconsin, and, I might add, brilliantly outlined – point by point, with receipts and all – by Dr. Peter Navarro in his three downloadable documents, "Immaculate Deception," "The Art of the Steal," and "Yes, President Trump Won: The Case, Evidence, & Statistical Receipts."

"Everyone in the world can now learn for themselves PRECISELY how the election was stolen from me and, moreover, STOLEN from my 74 million courageous MAGA voters by the feckless Democrats. With the help, of course, of fake news, Communist China, Big Tech, especially Zuckerberg at Facebook, and the Oligarchs on Wall Street.

"Of course, it's inexcusable how mainstream media has bluntly refused to acknowledge the greatest threat to truth, justice and rule of law in our long history as the beacon of integrity and freedom that we are.

"While it has long been understood, Alan, that the Democratic political apparatus engages in voter fraud, what changed this year was their relentless push to print and mail out tens of millions of ballots sent to unknown recipients with virtually no safeguards of any kind. This allowed fraud and abuse to occur in a scale never seen before, other than in places like North Korea, Somalia or Venezuela. Our election was a total catastrophe, and I cannot allow this to take place on my watch.

"The Democratic apparatus had this election rigged right from the beginning, Alan. They used the Wuhan bio-virus as an excuse to mail out tens of millions of ballots, which ultimately led to a big part of the fraud, a fraud that the whole world watched, and there is no one happier right now than the nuclear-armed, totalitarian genocidal leaders in Beijing, and their enablers in Silicon Valley and Wall Street, who want nothing more than to totally engulf our democracy with Communist state-capitalism and technocratic dictatorial rule. I will not let this travesty happen, Alan.

"Be clear, this election was about one thing: MASSIVE VOTER FRAUD; fraud that has never been seen like this in world history. The fact is, we WON the election without question. All over the country people know this. THE MEDIA KNOWS THIS as well, but they outright refuse to say it, because they know the result if they do. It's egregious and inexcusable, but that is what a corrupt media does.

"Even what I'm saying now to you, Alan, will be demeaned and disparaged and seen as EVIL, but fuck 'em. I'm going to see this through at all costs, because I'm not only representing the 74 million people who voted for me, I'm also representing all of the people who voted for my morally vacuous opponent, criminal Joe. And those hypocritical liars have proven many times again and again, that they will say, and do, anything to get back into power. But I tell you, Alan, MY FIGHT WILL HAVE NO MERCY AND IT HAS ONLY JUST BEGUN.

"Be clear: Donald J. Trump NEVER LOSES A FIGHT. HE NEVER GIVES UP. HE WILL NEVER SURRENDER.

HE WILL NOT BEND.

"BEING IMPEACHED and VILLIFIED IN THE MEDIA and BANNED ON FACEBOOK and TWITTER, WHO THE FUCK CARES with these petty annoyances? Why do I say this? Because I represent TRUTH and INTEGRITY and the SOUL OF ALL TRUE AMERICANS, and TOGETHER our hearts bleed red, white and blue.

"If they think I was hell to deal with in office, Alan, wait until I'm back at Mar-a-Lago and free of any constraints in the putrid swamp of Washington to inflict merciless maximum PAYBACK.

"I am going to turn my 128 room Palm Beach castle, what those jealous sell-outs call "The Grifter's Club," into a command bunker, and from there, inflict Armageddon. I've authorized missile strikes from Mar-a-Lago before, and I'll do it again, and MUCH, MUCH MORE.

FINDING TRUMP'S HEART

"Alan, you're on it," Bob encouraged me. "Transform the gentleman into the best version of himself. Unlike other political leaders, he has enough money and doesn't need more. Teach him the wisdom of the *Buddha* and *Dhamma*. INSPIRE the TRUE MAN in him to "Save America and the World too." Nurture the seeds of REDEMPTION and RECONCILIATION in him. It will be the greatest challenge of your life, but you can do it.

"Remember, despite it all, he is the ONLY ONE who will NOT SELL OUT TO THE C.C.P. and because of that, he's the ONLY ONE who can halt the DOOMSDAY CLOCK to save our species from killing ALL Life.

"As your archetypal warrior," Bob continued, "Donald will embrace your vision just as the Dalai Lama will, as well as his 74 million MAGA followers, in addition to many of Joe's own voters.

"No one wants to live like livestock. Just look at Xi Jinping's treatment of the Tibetans, the Uyghurs, and the people of Hong Hong. Be clear, the C.C.P. has an agenda of global domination and they know Biden will follow the money and not stand up to them.

"Draw upon your fifty years of mindfulness and *Dharma* teaching skills to inspire Donald – HERE at his greatest moment of need – to rise up and seize the highest expression of himself.

"So many of his G.O.P. colleagues have betrayed him," Bob continued. "The Globalists WANT TO CANCEL EVERY ASPECT OF HIS LIFE AND RID HISTORY OF HIS NAME AND ACCOMPLISHMENTS. STAND WITH HIM, Alan.

"It's bigger than Trump," Bob concluded. "This moment is about FREEDOM and TRUTH and FIGHTING FOR WHAT YOU BELIEVE IN, regardless of the odds. This is his Rocky moment. Help him embrace that part of you that also needs to be embraced. And remember, he'll love it, just as he loves Stallone."

I had never felt more optimistic as I brought TRUMP'S archetypal imagine back into focus, just as

I would a Buddhist-inspired visualization meditation; Donald J. Trump, as it were, a symbol of the *Bodhisattva* of Compassion, and a Buddha-to-be.

I entered the President's essence, flaws and all, and merged my heart with his own. This was my ultimate test of empathy-in-action.

"Alan, Nelson Mandela here from BLM in heaven. Remember, NO ONE is born hating another person because of the color of his skin, or his religion, or his political affiliation. Not even Donald J. Trump. People must learn to hate, just as Nancy Pelosi has and so many others within the Democratic Party. And if they can learn to hate, they can be taught to love, for love comes more naturally to the human heart than its opposite."

MY GOAL, I declared: Find TRUMP'S HEART – that place of innate love and goodness in each of us. Only then can we prevent an Oligarchic Take-Over – a Big Tech, C.C.P., Totalitarian, Wall Street, Biden, Davos ReSet, Capitalist coup.

We must heal, not divide, I reminded myself. We must foster national reconciliation and global freedom. We must bring hope to the PEOPLE and provide URGENT solutions on turning back the CLOCK on human generated extinction.

I got down on my knees in front of the large bronze Buddha statue from Burma in Bob's House of Rocky and committed myself to the greatest fight of my life

– inspiring President Donald J. Trump to embody his existential ROCKY.

"Alan, Stallone here. Mickey once told me before the BIG FIGHT: "Go for the ribs, don't let the bastard breathe." As much as Trump wishes he was me, we have to first humble him and show him how a real man fights.

"And before I go, one last thing, Alan. Before you get into the ring with this monster, remember, this is your own *Bodhisattva* moment; your own Par Lay and King and Gandhi all rolled in together. Go for it, dude. Leave nothing behind. You're going to eat lightning and crap thunder, just as I did in Rocky. It's now or never. Knock the ego out of the fucker and show him how to TRUELY BE A MAN and REALLY SAVE AMERICA and THE WORLD and HIMSELF TOO."

DON'T UNDERESTIMATE THEIR HATRED

I doubled down and fired UP. Integrating my meditative training with the LSD, I mindfully crafted a holographic image of DONALD J. TRUMP here inside of my heart within the sacred House of Rocky.

"Mr. President, I have a BIG IDEA for you. IT'S A GAME CHANGER. Not only can you have the presidency returned to you, you can become the GREATEST HUMAN that ever lived – the man who both resurrected the Constitutionality of the United States and saved our Great America and the world too from human generated extinction.

"Allow me to explain. We both know that the Chinese people have never enjoyed a day of freedom in their lives. As the Universal Declaration of Human Rights states, all people possess human rights and fundamental freedoms that governments must protect. The government of the People's Republic of China (P.R.C.), guided by a totalitarian ideology under the ABSOLUTE RULE of the Chinese Communist Party (C.C.P.), deprives citizens of their rights on a sweeping scale and systematically curtails freedoms as a way to retain power.

"Sadly, people in China cannot practice the religion or belief of their choice. They cannot express their opinions openly or form or join groups of their choosing without fear of harassment, arrest, or retribution. Members of minority groups are subject to mass arbitrary detention, Orwellian-style surveillance, political indoctrination, torture, forced abortions and sterilization, and state-sponsored forced labor.

"In short, the ruling Chinese Communist Party is a transnational criminal organization and BIG Tech, Corporate Media and the Oligarchs on Wall Street are in collusion with them. Why? Exactly, just as you have been saying, to build a ONE-PARTY GLOBAL SYSTEM. Throw in the collusion of the Biden Cartel and the world is doomed.

"Simply put, Sir, China is not only America's greatest enemy, they pose an existential threat to the world. And when you include their "weaponized C.C.P. bio-virus" and very likely, the more lethal viruses to come, they pose an existential threat to the very future of life.

"To combat the greatest threat our world has ever known, YOU, SIR, must immediately GO TO WAR with the TWIN EVILS – the genocidal Chinese communists and the cash guzzling Democratic globalists; Virus King Xi Jinping and his Titanic boy toy Captain Biden."

"Alan, Peter Sellers here from the "Magic Christian." You're doing great. And remember, 'everyone has their price' and Donald J. certainly has his, if you can find it, that is. In other words, feed him every line he wants to hear. Overall, stay calm and concentrated and mindful of course. And do another 100 micrograms of acid if needed. Take him to his knees. Then deliver 'here is your price to do as I say' punch."

"Let me cut to the chase, Mr. President," I continued. "You deserve PAYBACK. I don't mean ordinary revenge. I mean inflicting WICKED FURY on feckless Joe and his neoliberal morally repugnant running dogs, and especially those opportunistic Republicans like McConnell, Schumer, McCarthy, Newhouse, the slithering Liz Chaney, Romney, Barr, Bush, Tom Rice, Freddy boy Upton, Gonzales, Beutler, dough-boy Kristie, Kemp, Katko, Kitzinger, Meijer and Valadao. YUCK.

"And be sure, Sir, if you do not ACT NOW, these BIG

BROTHER pulled puppets with the cunning of the Titans on Wall Street and Silicon Valley will stop at nothing, until you, Mr. President, along with Pompeo, Giuliani, Bannon, Ivanka, Navarro, Eastman, and Jared, and sadly, Donald Jr. too, to name just a few, are ERASED FROM HISTORY, thrown down the memory hole, forever.

"I emphasize: Despite all their talk of unity, DO NOT underestimate their hatred for you. Many of them see you as a psychopathic Nazi white supremacist who should spend the rest of his life in prison, and the same for your family and friends too. They see you as an INSURRECTIONIST who attempted to overthrow America. They will not stop until you are locked away for the rest of your life.

"Sir, this is not easy to say. But you are a man of TRUTH and I feel this TRUTH coming through me. They will cram you into a windowless prison cell with Madoff, Cosby, and Weinstein, and force their perversity upon you. That's right, force the four of you into repeated acts of S&M porn. And probably web cam you to WARN others in the MAGA – DOMESTIC TERRORIST – movement that if they ever mention your name again, this will happen to them as well.

"As we know, Obama and Biden, despite their smiles, propagated a sadistic foreign policy that inflicted hell upon innocents in MANY countries, worldwide. Now, imagine what they'll do to you – a man they LOATHE, more than all the world's most despicable, combined. More than their hatred for Putin, Baghhdadi, Syria's Bashar al-Assad, Iran's Rouhani, and sadly, your Bro, Kim Jong-un in North Korea.

"After their first season of "gay prison porn," Sir, think castration, dick, balls, and all. They will then force you to take it in the rear from Cosby, on Quaalude's no less. And then force you to go down on Weinstein, as he spanks you, with a sound over of you chanting, "Four More Years." It's coming Sir, if you don't act, NOW.

"Please hear me out, Sir. Stealing the election from you was one thing, as was impeachment and a Senate trial, but REVENGE on the "Orange-haired Osama Bin Laden" will be of another order of magnitude altogether.

"Biden, Sir, may even force HBO to broadcast your incarceration and repeated rape as a "Trump torture-porn reality show." There is no doubt that they want your 74 million followers to LOSE ALL HOPE and cower in fear, until they SELF-DESTRUCT in utter despair, ultimately erased from history.

"With your infamy, Sir, as the most misunderstood, yet most hated man in the history of America, "Trump Really Reality Prison Theater" may be bigger than even Season 8 of the "Game of Thrones." And let's not forget that HBO is owned by none-other than your favorite corporation, Warner Media. And the proud owner of CNN. That's right! Think Jack Clapper and Anderson Looper offering blow by blow analysis of each episode."

"Wait, wait, Alan" Mr. Trump says.

As the President gets on the speaker phone and calls for Pompeo, Mnuchin, Ivanka, Melania, Navarro, Eastman, Jared, Giuliani and Bannon – to come into his office immediately – I tweak the clarity of my life-transforming *Mandala* – my self-generated interactive meditation on conquering evil through self-love, reconciliation, and unconditional unity.

As Trump's inner circle enters the Oval Office – one by one – I suck it up and embrace their essential humanness in my acid-accentuated field of loving kindness and empathy; feeling them as I would family – as sacred beings in my own *Samsaric Sangha*.

I strengthened my resolve by reflecting on the words of His Holiness the 14th incarnation of the Dalai Lama of Tibet, instructing all HUMAN BEINGS to always include the most EVIL people in our lives as 'UN-OWNED ASPECTS OF OURSELVES and SYMBOLIC OF THE SACRED UNITY OF ALL THINGS.' And when in doubt, INCLUDE, INCLUDE, and INCLUDE THAT PERSON TOO, no exceptions.

As his innermost allies stood in silence in a semi-circle around the President, Mr. Trump broke my reflection stating in a tone of unexpected warmth, "I'm sorry if I interrupted your flow, Alan, please continue."

"Mr. Trump, allow me to repeat myself and in

somewhat of a crass manner, to emphasize the point for your family and friends: I am genuinely sorry the election was stolen from you. These meat puppets led by the Biden Cartel and that porn obsessed crack addict son, Hunter, are, as you know, CRIMINALS in the pocket of China's soul-sucking Dictator Xi Jinping and his 90-million-member Totalitarian Communist Party of genocidal cyborgs. Clearly, they must be STOPPED.

"What Xi did in Hong Kong imprisoning Jimmy Lai, Joshua Wong, Wu Chi-wai, and EVERY OTHER pro-democracy activist is PURE EVIL, and Biden did not say a word about it. You on the other hand, Sir, stood up and spoke out. Yet you are reviled as a fascist freedom hater.

"Further, what China's Mao did to Tibet in 1951 with the genocide of 2.5 million Tibetans is a crime against God and Humanity. And it continues today. Biden and the Democrats say nothing. Again, you had the moral courage to speak out.

"And now that Xi has Biden and his corporate crime syndicate cronies down on all fours, they will not stop their full-scale incarceration of the free world until we are all slave laborers for the C.C.P.

"In short: as you know, Sir, fear exists in our brains. Whereas honor, dignity and liberty live in our hearts. You have both heart, Sir, and leadership. And our precious world will come to an END unless you use both your heart and leadership and NOW. And, I may add, you clearly deserve the Nobel Peace Prize, and with my plan, I am confident that you'll win it."

A VISION FOR A FREE WORLD

"THE PLAN: As you know, Sir, Davos, Switzerland, is the home of the World Economic Forum. Their mission: "We, the Global Elite, as the proud fascist caretakers of the world, stand committed to our ongoing subjugation of all peoples and destruction of the planet, by coercing business, political, and religious leaders to collude with us to co-create an unsustainable and dystopian future, as we continue to profit.

"Hold your reaction, Sir. Just making a point and if you would, please allow me to keep developing it.

"We know, Sir, that you spoke at their conference last year and addressed the who's who in criminal sociopathy, corporate fraud, money laundering, tax evasion, and collectively, the most despicable leaders in the world.

"But sadly, Sir, none of them could hear your plea TO SAVE THE WORLD through global ethics, nuclear disarmament, zero-emissions by 2025, and economic equality the world over, especially for those traumatized regions raped for their resources and slave labor to enhance the wealth of the Elites.

"And my God, Mr. Trump, look at how these planet-destroying neocolonialist imperialist Jihadists expressed their gratitude. They threw you under the bus, poured gasoline all over your Brioni suit, and immolated you with a stolen election, yet another trial, another impeachment, and escalated their VILIFICATION of you and the entire MAGA movement to FULL SCALE DEMONIZATION in the corporate media. And now, identifying you as a domestic terrorist. A CRIMINAL. Shame on them."

Mr. Trump and family glanced at each other with thoughts of possibly being conned. But I assured them with several mindful waves of unconditional loving kindness, and they were disarmed.

"Mr. President," I continued, "allow me to remind you. The very chair you are sitting on is the most favorite chair of my dear friend Robert Chartoff. I think you had him over for dinner back in the day in Manhattan. You will remember, Bob is the renowned Oscar winning producer of thirty-nine Hollywood films, including your favorite, "Rocky." Similar to you, he grew up poor in New York and made it big.

"Few know that Bob was a long-time meditator and, in fact, after we travelled to Burma, he introduced mindfulness to Hollywood and the movie industry with our day long retreats at his Malibu home. I married Bob and his wife, Jenny. Bob always told me, "Everyone deserves a second chance," and to NEVER GIVE UP in one's pursuit of GREATNESS.

"Mindfulness is the key word here, Sir, to achieving your DREAM. From my humble experience, all good comes from it and I'm here to assist you in developing "mindful intelligence" – the next iteration of this transformational, freedom-enhancing quality to actualize your full potential.

"My VISION is this: Bring unmindful Joe and his cabal of "never ending lose-yet-another-war" globalists together as they do annually in Davos, lorded over by King Creep Klaus, and create a "Clockwork Orange-like-transformation-conversion-experience" to rid them of their proclivity for corporate TOTALITARIANISM, driven by their fetish for PROFIT over the preservation of nature and the planet.

"Through a highly advanced AI version of "trauma-releasing self-hatred conversion therapy" developed by our beloved visionary Elon Musk, along with my input, you can PURGE them of EVIL and STOP their diabolical death wish to keep the Doomsday Clock Tik Toking, as well as remove their repulsive desire to make the people of our great country peasant slave laborers for the totalitarian C.C.P., and Wall Street, of course.

"As your Deep State Intel has revealed, together with the Biden regime, the C.C.P. is forming the Fourth Reich. And we thought Hitler was wickedly hypnotic. We may as well be livestock under the C.C.P.-Biden Joint Totalitarian Venture, AKA, let's Destroy America and the World too, and give everyone $1,400 to survive for yet another "do as we say, stay at home" month, as we print our TRILLIONS and prepare for a world with you as our permanent slaves.

"With your background as a self-made billionaire and the finest President of our Great Republic, you're the only human with the masculinity, moral courage and compassion required to preserve the very soul of our great Declaration of Independence, that states: "We hold these truths to be self-evident, that all men, and only White men, are created equal; that they are endowed by their White Creator with certain inalienable White Only Rights, that among these are Life, Liberty, Golf, Wealth, Whiteness, and the Pursuit of Happiness."

"Setting aside the humor, I propose that you produce, Sir, a new version of Davos called "Davos-X To Save The World."

"With the help of Mr. Mnuchin here, our beloved former-Secretary of the Treasury, who is the GRAND-MASTER OF MONEY, we have a winner. Of course, with his long family history as PARTNERS IN GOLDMAN SACHS, he has the lowdown on EVERYONE with criminal power in the world.

"With the two of you working together, we have our Micky–Stallone, ROCKEY MOMENT. I know Mnuchin here is not all that fond of you anymore, but he wants to be sure he has a future out of prison, if you know what I mean.

"Davos-X can also be held in Switzerland. We can also do this virtually, if preferred. The goal of D-X is to rub the faces of these neoliberal globalists in their blood lust for money, power, and privilege. And thereby, purge them of their pathology of MORE IS ALWAYS BETTER, and thus overcome their planet destroying sociopathic ways and immediately have you back in office, the latest in 2024.

"We also want them to honor you as the only man who can save America and the world from the C.C.P.'s evil plot for global totalitarianism and sadly, the final domino towards societal collapse, nuclear war, mass starvation, and near-term extinction.

"We want the Globalists to say, we APOLGIZE FOR VILIFYING YOU. We also want them to thank you, Mr. Donald J. Trump, for making a stand to defend freedom, unity and the inherent dignity of the working class. And moreover, not only keeping your promise of Making America Great, but also MAKING the WORLD GREAT by MAKING NATURE more primary than PROFIT."

Mr. Trump and Mr. Mnuchin and family are smiling with receptivity, as Mr. Trump says, "Please continue, Alan. I think we're close to a deal."

"Like a Global Ted-X, Davos-X will be an elite international event and have the world leaders salivating to be invited. We will bill D-X as "The Ultimate Planet Saving Gathering On Earth", to call off the consumerist war on nature, end the human fetish for fossil fuels, and STOP the death march to Armageddon.

"Everyone will want to be part of your creation towards more sustainable behaviors in order to preserve the sanctity of both human and non-human life.

"Even "forgot my name" Joe will be humbled and kindly ask Mr. Mnuchin to allow him participation. After all, once a sell-out, always new horizons to conquer.

"Of course, Davos-X is a ploy, Sir, to get the Totalitarian Oligarchs all in one spot for you to then deliver your KNOCKOUT PUNCH.

"As the master of entrepreneurship that you are, you can easily pull this off. And I'm certain, Sir, that after the obscenity of them stealing the election, impeaching and criminalizing you, payback is more important than anything at this point. Right?"

Trump shakes his head in agreement and then calmly asks, "What's in it for you? How much do you want out of this?"

"Nothing, Sir, my only interest is in helping you return to office and to seek maximum revenge in the process. As an American patriot, I also want to help you Make America and the World Great Again and prevent us from falling under the grip of totalitarianism.

"See, I lived in Burma under military dictatorship and saw the evil it inflicts upon the people. I am also an American. My parents were both veterans of WWII. Although you have flaws, we all do, of course. But you, Sir, respect democracy and universal human rights and the global elite's worship totalitarianism, slavery and the death of nature.

"By the way, I lost several friends and donors by expressing even a hint of support for you."

"What," Trump fires back, "how is that?"

"As I said, Sir, you can be obnoxious, even a pain in the ass at times. It's not easy for any of us to overcome our narcissism. I know, none of us want to hear that, but it's true. I can even be difficult at times, and that's after decades of intensive meditation, mindfulness, *yoga* and ardent spiritual practice.

"You, on the other hand, have done nothing much of anything to actualize your true self, as far as I can see. No breathwork. No *yoga*. No plant medicine. No meditation. No psychedelic-assisted psychotherapy. No mindfulness training, although you did support our troops learning mindfulness to kill more effectively and without regret. That's why we're moving on to "mindful intelligence", now.

"My point: you have a personality disorder, as I do, and that makes us indifferent to others' feelings a lot of the time. In addition, you say a lot of mean things about others. And you come across as grotesquely entitled a lot of the time, etc etc.

"Frankly, I have no idea how Melania deals with you. But hey, you're the President and the far better choice over C.C.P sell out, disoriented Joe. And so I made that choice sort of clear to some of my friends.

"But still, they thought I had lost it and some of them shamed me and stopped supporting my work. Some even tried to ruin my career, especially the Buddhists; back biting, spreading lies, saying I was a drug and sex addict, had no boundaries, lies, lies, and more lies. All weak and jealous actors, like follow-the-money Joe.

"Others chalked up my support for you to yet another symptom of my early childhood brain trauma.

"Frankly, I even tried to explain to them that evil CNN – who vilifies you nonstop, as we know – is owned by, yep, Warner Media. And Warner is owned by AT & T. And AT & T is Chaired by none other than Randal Stephenson, up until a few days ago, that is. Who, as you may know, was the former Chair of the Boy Scouts of America from 2016 to 2018. Sound suspicious? I know, it brings up names like George Pell and Pope Francis.

"Now, I don't like to make false accusations, but one wonders why 100,000 sexual abuse cases were filed by boys before, during and after Randal's watch as Chair. Is it that AT & T is the media's equivalent of the Catholic Church?"

"Are you saying," Trump asks, "that CNN and Warner and AT & T are child trafficking and likely to be involved in the pedophile ring of Epstein, Clinton, Soros, and many of the other Global elites?"

"Well, Sir, I'm not a closet QAnon conspirator, but let me say, I want to help you make the world a safer place. And let us not forget that Warner also owns HBO, who, of course, produced "Game of Thrones." And what they did to institutionalize and normalize "torture-rape" tells it all.

"Let me conclude by saying, these Democrats love their "forever wars" and the massacring of millions in the name of privilege and corporate profits. Although Jeffrey and Hunter are sexual psychopaths, they're small players. But President Obama, Biden's Daddy, was a proud fan of the Game of Groans that spit in the face of the Me Too Movement with its gratuitous sexual violence.

"What does that tell you about a leader? And to think his wife – "When They Go Low We Go High" – called you monstrous and pleaded for you to be banned from social media, and he had the audacity to crucify you for your so-called misogamy and sexual assaults. Talk about the pot calling the kettle black.

"And let us not forget, Sir, millions of men went to war for Hitler and millions of women wished to have his child. It will take some work to convert these totalitarian deviants, but if we don't try, it's the END."

Trump looked towards his family for clues to determine his own course of action. The room is pregnant with silence and amplified with life and death pressure. The President then looks firmly into the eyes of his daughter and asks, "What do you think, Ivanka?"

Ivanka doesn't answer. Rather, she turns her gaze towards the stunning Louise Linton – Steven Mnuchin's 39-year-old uber-sexy, super-cool, uninhibited movie star wife – as she undulates into the room and Ivanka asks, "What do you think, babe?"

Louise turns her sultry gaze to me and with the most seductive *Mara*-like smile says, "I've been listening to you on speaker, and I'd say it's a deal if Alan agrees to let me dance at D-X and also turn the weekend into a feature film to be released after my new film, "Me You Madness.""

Louise then sits down on the husband's lap as her mini-skirt flirts with her upper thighs and kisses her husband with all of her sexiness and when done, asks, "Will you produce the film for us, love? We can make it under our brought-back-to-life RatPac label and get either Fox or Warner to finance it, just as we did with Avatar, Mad Max, and American Sniper."

Mnuchin unhesitatingly smiles in full agreement and Louise turns to her sister Ivanka and winks, 'yes.' Ivanka then turns to the President and says, "Dad, I grew up with your most favorite quote on my bedroom wall. Let me remind you of the words of our revolutionary brother, Nobel Peace Laureate, Andrei Sakharov."

"That's okay dear," Trump responds. And with a smile of respect, he says to his beloved daughter, "I remember well the words of our great spokesperson for the conscience of humankind." And just as Mr. Trump was about to recite the quote, everyone in the room stood and, while saluting the American flag, recited the quote word for word, in perfect harmony.

"Intellectual freedom is essential – freedom to obtain and distribute information, freedom for open-minded and un-fearing debate, and freedom from pressure by officialdom and prejudices. Such freedom of thought is the only guarantee against an infection of people by mass myths, which, in the hands of treacherous hypocrites and demagogues, can be transformed into bloody dictatorship."

President Trump reached out his hand for a shake and with a smile said, "You've got a deal, Mr. Clements."

DAVOS-X

"Here's how we do it, Sir. Between yourself – the most powerful man in the world – AND Mr. 'Goldman Sachs' Mnuchin here, along with your diehard loyalists at the CIA, you know everyone with privilege and power the world over, and moreover, have the lowdown on their shenanigans.

"None of them, Sir, will want those highly classified files dropped that you're taking to Mar-a-Lago, with those damning emails, videos, and phone recordings that show their true DARKNESS. What you can do to ruin lives would make Wikileaks look like Sunday in Church. By way of saying, and as you know so well, 'EVERYONE HAS A PRICE.' Especially sold-out Political Leaders and the Corporate Oligarchs with their Cabal of Wall Street Cronies they collude with.

"And what an opportunity to PAY BACK that fascistic and unmindful Jack Dorsey for his inexcusable "permanent suspension" of your Twitter account, and that of Bannon too. All for what? Your LOVE OF AMERICA AND FREEDOM OF EXPRESSION?

"You are the President of the United States of America, for God's sake. It's unforgivable.

"And say no more about cyborg Zuck at Give-Me-China-book for his collusion with Daddy B and the C.C.P. In fact, all those Tech Titan twits will have their day of reckoning at Davos-X.

"Even your friend KJ-un will come over on his nuked-powered jet, as will your archenemy – DIC-XI of China. Even Pope Francis will not want to miss out. And no doubt, Jeffrey E. will come out of hiding on Orgy Island and jet in wearing a face mask of Saudi King Abdullah's perverted son, Prince Majed Al-Saud, to maintain maximum anonymity.

"Bill will most certainly buy a few dozen passes for the likes of his blood-lusting cult buddies, the Rothschild's, Soros, and Prince A, that is, if they can be persuaded to break for a week from their Adrenochrome parties, drained from their kidnapped kids. Of course, Bono of U2 will pray to perform, as will Pope Francis, Snoop Dogg and Stephen Colbert. You'll be turning away the stars, Sirs.

"Once there and everyone is settled, you give the opening presentation and explain that you have had a radical spiritual conversion and want to share it with them by taking them on the ultimate journey of their lives to inspire their highest most compassionate commitment to the SURVIAL OF LIFE and the preservation of NATURE. They'll be in AWE.

And of course, some will think, WTF? You assure them that due to all the unfortunate events of the recent past, you have discovered the WISDOM OF UNITY and the NECESSITY OF RECONCILIATION. Your radical contrition and spiritual rebirth will blow their minds and open their dark hearts.

"With their unexpected receptivity, you explain that you wish to take them on a special spiritual adventure, called TANKA-X, that is grounded, of all things, in MINDFULNESS – the NEW RELIGION OF THE BIDEN ADMINISTRATION. With that, they will drop in reverence.

"This mind-expanding heart opening experience, Sir, is designed by our beloved AI expert Elon Musk, with input from his Holiness the Dalai Lama, Elie Wiesel, Rabbi Spero, Archbishop Desmond Tutu, T.D. Jakes, Oprah, and myself.

"Our goal, Sir, is to provide the mindful intelligence, the essential guidance and inspiration, for everyone to design concrete plans with clear time frames and make FIRM commitments to implement actions to SAVE the WORLD from catastrophic collapse.

"We will emphasize the URGENCY to make the

planet primary, full stop. Action, Action, Action, as Mr. Bannon likes to say. But first our BELOVED D-Xers must be convinced there's a problem. This will be handled by TANKA-X.

"Your goal, Sir, and the mission of Davos-X, is: NOT ONLY are we committed to STOPPING the Doomsday Clock, BUT TURNING IT BACK AN HOUR. With this in mind, we will implement a world class training to cease our hedonistic addiction to consumerism, the key issue that must be addressed by all world leaders and nations, AT ONCE.

"I can see that you are having some doubts, Mr. Trump. But rest assured, no one worth their global elitist status will want to miss this historic Earth saving event, and frankly, I see no other way to return to the White House nor channel your FURY in the most conscious manner, at the very people who threw you under the bus."

"Carry on, Alan, please. Yes, I WANT MAXIMUM PAYBACK."

"In your opening remarks, Sir, you can include a few lines from our courageous Greta Thunberg's address at the United Nations. This will inspire credibility and build trust, as participants will be MOVED by your humility, seeing that you've done a 180 on your insulting statements towards our beloved eco-activist.

"NOT to worry, Sir, we can put all this on a teleprompter, if you wish to save the stress of memorizing it.

"You can start by saying, "This is all wrong. I should not be up here. I should be back in Mar-a-Lago on the other side of the ocean grooving with my wife and fellow wealthies. Do you know that more Americans have died from Covid than those brave souls that perished in World War I, II and Vietnam combined? Yet, you all come to us Covid survivors for hope. How dare you!

"Let me remind you, you have stolen my dreams of a second term with your anger, insults and lies, and ruined my plans to make America and the world great. And yet I'm one of the lucky ones. I have billions of dollars, a beautiful wife and family, and the protection of the secret service along with numerous luxury properties, hotels and golf courses, around the world.

"Yet, millions of people are suffering at this very moment. Yes, people are dying everywhere. Entire ecosystems are collapsing. Get it, we are in the beginning of the sixth mass extinction, and all you can talk about is your hatred of me, referring to me as Hitler, wanting to REMOVE ME FROM HISTORY, along with your obsession with money, privilege, Wall Street, global control, and your pathetic GREEN fairy tales of eternal economic growth.

"Do you not know that GREEN GROWTH is an oxymoron? Do you NOT KNOW you have spread POISONS ALL OVER THE WORLD? Do you NOT KNOW YOU HAVE TURNED OUR OCEANS INTO PLASTIC? DO

YOU NOT REALIZE YOUR DEATH WISH? All for what? Let's destroy the world to increase our wealth? How dare you!"

"And you go on, Sir, to hammer the point home: "For more than thirty years the science on climate collapse has been crystal clear. How dare you continue to look away and come here saying that you're doing enough, when the politics and solutions needed to prevent the Apocalypse are still nowhere in sight."

"Now, Sir, you are free to soar. Lay it on them. Tell 'em like it is: "Our earthly house is on fire. It's burning with your fucking greed and stupidity, and you say that you hear me and that you understand the urgency. Fuck you. Capitalism must end or capitalism will end us. But no matter how pissed off I get, you all still play dumb. Because if you really understood the situation, as I explained so clearly in my four years in office, and if you still fail to act, then you would be evil. And despite the fact that you are evil, I refuse to believe it."

"At that point, Sir, your wife, Jared, Navarro, Mayor Giuliani and Stephan K. Bannon, and others in your inner circle, hand out head coverings; Space-X-like high tech masks, designed by Elon, of course. Since everyone has been vaccinated, there is no fear of the Wuhan bio-virus, so the head coverings are to personalize TANKA-X for each person. EACH mask is CUSTOM made to the head of each D-Xer and outfitted with the AI-driven 4-D holographic imaging, to maximize the realism of the journey they're about to go on.

"The excitement in the conference room is palatable as U2 cranks, "Bullet The Blue Sky" followed by Rage Against The Machine's masterpiece in non violence, "Killing In the Name."

And all participants came prepared, showered, and wearing their organic hand-spun Egyptian cotton "Davos-X To Save the World" black lounge robes, designed for each person, and generously donated by your friend Michael Lindell at "My Pillow."

"The room is secured and, unbeknownst to the nature killing elitists, each person is administered a high dose of vaporized AI-created psychedelic within their head gear. Of course, we'll have highly trained psychedelic-assisted psychiatrists on board to assist should anyone need a second dose or show resistance to the mindfulness-based self-hatred conversion therapy.

"I'll also be there to help anyone who truly begins to crack, and perhaps wants to jump out a window or threatens to slice their wrists from accessing an excessive amount of trauma from the moral shame of recognizing their soulless past. Of course, we do not want any self-harm to compromise the success of the event nor give the media fodder for negative coverage.

"Their automatized lounge chairs are then lowered back, and each person feels as if they are in zero gravity.

Each of their Davos-X robes were tailored made and wired with the infamous high tech OM sensors that not only know far more about the person than they know about themselves, it also adjusts bodily temperature to a perfect comfort level second by second.

"As the psychedelic comes on, their normally one-dimensional minds become as granular as parachuting is real. As Lao Tzu said, Sir, "the journey of 1000 miles begins with the first step," and thus begins the ultimate Clockwork Orange-like transformational conversion therapy experience ever conceived to rid consciousness of narcissism, authoritarianism and any desire for meat.

"On the 4-D screens in their mind's eye, they see a holographic real-life experience unfolding. Thanks again to Elon and his team of scientific savants, it's impossible to not see one's experience as REAL and FEEL it as TRUE, as in actually occurring in real time. So much so, one instantly loses any reference point that it is in fact a fiction – a trans-humanism OM generated AI illusion.

"By the way, Sir, you will be given an honorary 1,000,000 shares of OM before it goes public soon after you resume the Presidency, as will your wife, family and your closet circle of friends."

As I come out of my meditation, I reminded myself, stay grounded, Alan. This is a manifestation of your own mind – symbols of your own inner *Mandala* – your own

War with *Samsara*. Stay focused on your mission: why stay alive and adapt to the horror of the sixth mass extinction?

GODDESS IVANKA

"As the psychedelic intensifies, our D-Xers merge into their personalized inner-cinemas; seeing spectacular images of Mother nature, they hear Sir Richard Attenborough narrate these breathtaking glimpses of snow-capped peaks, deep blue oceans with whales surfacing; a crystal clear river with salmon jumping; into a lush forest with a family of mountain gorillas; an eagle soaring in the blue sky of freedom; and outward – the orbiting of Earth from 300 miles high – as if they themselves were viewing HOME from outer space, while suspended in zero gravity.

"Each D-Xer's heart softens, and their mind expands. And with each breath they feel an unexpected re-enchantment with the natural world, that slowly subverts their subconscious identities motivated by greed, domination and profit, while beginning to see themselves as a driver in a "homicidal economy."

"Suddenly, from within a sunbeam appears a rainbow of colors, and out of the spectrum emerges your beautiful daughter, Ivanka. She stands tall – poised in her elegance, while making intimate eye contact with each Davosian. They are spellbound by the unexpected and her unparalleled charm and beauty, Sir.

"As she mindfully and slowly undresses, revealing her erotic black lingerie, Ivanka engages each D-Xer with the most intimate heart of pure loving kindness. She in turn becomes the most angelic *tantric* Goddess each man has ever met. Their defenses relax and their hearts open –MDMA-like.

"Speaking of which, Sir. I brought some ecstasy for you and your family and friends. I know you don't do drugs, so like the psychedelic for the D-Xers this too is an AI generated placebo and, frankly, works far better than the real thing. It's so pure and joyful, it's like hitting a hole in one three holes in a row, or if the election results were overturned and you return to the White House soon or, NO WORRIES, even if you have to wait until 2024. Here, take it with a glass of water. It's utterly harmless.

"As we know, Elon has the very best taste in women, and he and his team have assured me that they have spared nothing to create the ultimate virtual girlfriend experience for each D-Xer. Of course, participants do not realize that Ivanka, like you and me, see these dastardly men as the leading members of the Fourth Reich and the ideologues destroying the world.

"As we know so well, Sir, people do not voluntarily change. We can't jail them or give them all lobotomies. So what we are doing here with TANKA-X is creating the ultimate conversion experience, Sir, that will inflict the maximum psychological transformation for each of them.

And allow you the BLISS of REVENGE, and much more: a most certain return to the presidency."

IVA-FRANCESKA

"Nor do they know, Sir, that your beloved daughter Ivanka has become a renowned human rights activist. Inspired, no less, by one of the world's most heroic selfless Jewish woman, Franceska Mann – the stunningly beautiful Polish ballerina, born February 4, 1917, and who died twenty-six years later.

"Ivanka only recently discovered, in a past life regression session, that she was, in fact, the reincarnation of Franceska. She learned that during the rise of one of the Global elite's founding fathers, Adolf Hitler and his glorious Third Reich, Franceska was captured, thrown into the Warsaw Ghetto, resisted, captured again, and taken to Auschwitz.

"According to legend, Franceska, like yourself, Sir, wanted to pay back her captors – those White supremacist German officers gleefully exterminating Jews and other deplorables by day, cutting their eyes and organs out after sexually humiliating them at night.

"Franceska convinced the camp commandant to let her offer a striptease to the SS officers to offset the stress of extermination and give them a spiritually rejuvenating performance they would never forget.

"We could say, this was Franceska's "Rocky" moment.

It was certainly a night in Auschwitz that was unknown in any detail, until a recording was recently discovered in a hidden vault in the basement of German Chancellor Angela Merkel's home in Berlin.

"Even fewer people know that after a private showing of the film to the Norwegian Nobel Peace Prize Committee, they posthumously bestowed Franceska with the prestigious prize.

"What happened was, due to unrelenting international pressure driven by the neoliberal fascists and their propaganda wing – mainstream corporate media – the Nobel Committee was forced to revoke Aung San Suu Kyi's prize, awarded for her nonviolent challenge to military dictatorship, and since they had a free one, they gave it to Franceska. And no doubt, Sir, once the world learns that Ivanka is Franceska's embodiment, she too will go on to be awarded the prize as well.

"Let me continue, please. Because Franceska was known to be the most beautiful and sexiest woman in Poland, all the Reich elites came to Auschwitz to see her perform. This included such luminaries as Hermann Göring – Commander and Chief of Luftwaffe, the German Air Force, and the principle architect of the gas chambers; Reichsführer-SS Heinrich Himmler, one of the main visionaries of the Holocaust itself; SS Lieutenant Colonel Rudolf Hoess – the Senior Commandant of Auschwitz, who managed to show up, forcing himself to break from his experimental operations on the fetuses of pregnant women without anesthesia, no less; SS Major Richard Baer – Senior Commander of neighboring Birkenau, who broke away from his gassing duties and drove over; even Klaus "the Butcher of Lyon" Barbie, the undisputed greatest sadist ever born, alongside Hitler himself, placed a 24 hour halt on his fetish for vaginal mutilation and came out.

"No one wanted to miss Poland's most gifted Jewish dancer offer a one-off private sex show that would, of course, be kept secret from the wives and children of the Senior SS officials, lest their morality be publicly sullied on national television and in the mainstream press.

A NIGHT TO REMEMBER IN AUSCHWITZ

"As Franceska stripped and danced on the makeshift stage at the Auschwitz Underground Burlesque Theater, other young naked luscious Jewish women – not yet emaciated by starvation and traumatized by gang rape – mingled with the Senior Officials and made sure the vodka and LSD were freely flowing.

"As Franceska put her cleanly shaven pussy in the face of each senior officer in the front row, the sexually charged energy electrified the smoke-filled space. And as the evening unfolded the SS men were seen salivating, lusting with fantasies for this gorgeous goddess's fully naked undulating perfectly white angelic Jewish body.

"Each time an SS white cultist reached forward to touch her dripping wet vagina, or leaned forward to smell the fragrance of her 'everyone has their price' for pussy and profit, she politely smiled and pulled back, but kept dancing.

"She was breathtakingly mindful to empathize with the men's desires as natural to the deviant white pigs they were. After all, she reasoned, these men were victims too. They were once perfect white boys who were taught by perfect white parents to destroy their perfect white empathy.

"And now," she said, "I'll give you back your camp law: 'Us Jews going to our death must be deceived to the very end. This is the only permissible form of charity.'" And as her mercy grew, she squatted and thrust open her legs, pushing her sacred *yoni* a few inches from the cold stone face of the senior Commandant of the camp. With an eroticized wink and nod, she invited him to lick her dripping wet pussy.

"Time stopped. Everyone in the room got up and gathered around the Commandant. After mindfully taking off his SS hat, he mindfully leaned forward and with an outstretched tongue he mindfully closed one eye... and just as he was to enter her and lose all sense of his genocidal self, Franceska grabbed his pistol and shoved it in his mouth and blew his brains out the back of his head.

"She then emptied the remaining bullets into the

frenzied faces of as many of those deranged white supremacist pigs as she could, in a blazing fire of existential bliss.

"Instantly, five black hooded SS men stood over
Franceska and emptied hundreds of bullets into every
inch of her naked body, especially into her pussy, as if to
make the point: we hate our fear of the feminine and WE
LOVE DEATH.

"To make God quiver, Klaus Barbie ordered a massive
German Shepard guard dog to do Franceska in her rear,
while the remaining SS leaders cheered and clapped and
danced and guzzled vodka in white supremacist delight.

"The dog was then ordered to eat Franceska's mangled remains. Thus, the legend of Franceska was born,
and perhaps the greatest and most creative freedom fighter the world has never known."

IVA EMBRACES HER DIVINE FEMININE

I came back to the House of Rocky and then dropped back
into the narrative at hand: "Mr. Trump, your genius daughter, Ivanka, as I explained, does her version of our Nobel
Peace laureate, Franceska Mann, at Davos-X. But this time
the tables are turned: You, Sir, are the Commandant of
D-X – an anti-Auschwitz analogy – to pay back the trolls
of the neoliberal morally vacuous Fourth Reich and the
Global Oligarchs who puppet them.

"They see a life-like AI 4-D creation of Ivanka – who
is really Louise Linton, Mnuchin's uninhibited seductress

wife – slowly stripping to the favorite music of each Davosian channeled Clockwork Orange-like into their sociopathic, nature-hating, life-destroying soullessness. Hence, the "ultimate OM-inspired transformational self-hatred conversion therapy" begins. And with each passing minute boundaries erode, defenses relax, and the denial of each D-Xer further cracks WIDE OPEN.

"While Ivanka channels Franceska, Louise moves with transcendental tantric grace, and further entices each D-Xer in their mind's third eye – to let go, trust, OPEN and love, so beautifully illuminated by the psyche-delic and OM's 4-D optics.

"Let me explain another important fact, Mr. Trump: Ivanka is not only the reincarnation of Franceska; Franceska is the reincarnation *Avalokiteshvara*, the *Bodhisattva* of Compassion, who just happens to be the next *Buddha*. That's right, your very own daughter.

"Ava," as she is known in ancient Indian culture, is a *Tantric* Goddess and the archetypal expression of the Divine Feminine. Ava fearlessly manifests her embodied wisdom on the life canvas of uncontrived freedom.

"Together – Ivanka, Franceska and Ava – are one and the same spirit and the hidden esoteric meaning of Notre Dame. The Great Woman of Paris is none other than the universal archetype of the DIVINE FEMININE (aka DF).

"DF pervades every dimension of the meta-sphere, including black holes and worm holes and galaxies far and near, unifying all dualities, wherever found. In the absence of DF in human men, they perversely bond through war, murder and rape, both of women and underage girls, and desecrate nature herself.

"Even in more relaxed times, men with insufficient DF act out their degenerative impulses on such websites as Pornhub, X-Tube and Spank-Wire.

"In addition, such DF-deficient men often hide their true natures behind the veil as politicians and priests, even presidents and prime ministers, and in some cases even as popes. But beneath their veneer of civility, Sir, they are pedophiles, predators, and planetary destroying perverts. In short, "Divine Feminine Deficit Disorder" is why America is a mess and we are currently in a mass extinction event.

"On the other side, DF energy, Sir, is the most healing live-giving source of dignity throughout the ten known dimensions of the universe, and of course throughout nature herself. Those men with high levels of DF prefer women as leaders, even presidents and prime ministers and priestesses.

"With really high levels of DF, such men call for the absolute end of men in all key roles in society, including politicians, bankers, CEOs, hedge fund managers, brokers, even prime ministers and presidents, and not withstanding such superfluous jobs as online *yoga* and meditation and mindfulness teachers, and even Zoom based shamans, coaches and psychotherapists as well.

"An enlightened expression of DF is experienced, Mr. Trump, as the absolute transcendence of good and evil and arrival at the primordial UNITY of ALL THINGS. By way of saying, your precious Ivanka – soon to be the Governor of Florida – is the living embodiment of the Divine Feminine. And with the skillful acting of our amazing Louise, and her RatPac film crew, we will soon have you back in office, along with what we hope to be an Oscar winning feature film, documenting the greatest transformation in human history."

"Amazing, Alan. I like it. I want to call it "The House of Rocky." Now, before we go on, please tell me more about Pornhub. I want to be sure that Davos-X is not in any way related. People accuse me, as you did, of being a misogamist, but it's all propaganda. Yes, I am pro-life, but that's my belief in the right to life. And by the way, I hated "Game of Thrones" for their despicable portrayal of women being brutally stripped and raped, and then hiding behind that bullshit excuse of wanting to "remain authentic to medieval times." Anyway, please tell me about Pornhub."

"Pornhub, Sir, just as Dominion Voting Systems, is a Canadian based Company. Pornhub is owned by Mindgeeks and is based in Montreal. It has 3.5 billion visitors a month; more than Netflix, Amazon or Yahoo.

"Pornhub is the 10th most visited site in the world.

Surveys have shown that Pornhub's ten million hours of video has had the fourth greatest impact on society in the 21st century. Just after you, and after its competitors Facebook and Google, but ahead of rivals Apple, Amazon and Microsoft.

"Frankly, Sir, it's unimaginable that Canada's Prime Minster, Justin Trudeau, a declared feminist and an apologist for the neoliberals, allows Pornhub to operate in his country. Which, I might add, is infested with rape videos, and monetizes child sodomy, revenge pornography, spy cam videos of women forced to do inconceivable things, and toxic misogynist content, and even footage of women being asphyxiated in plastic bags.

"I can assure you, Mr. Trump, that our creation in Davos-X is what Elon and I call "anti-porn" and will offer the world a much need training in accessing one's latent Divine Feminine to safeguard the sanctity of freedom and the preservation of Nature, and all life itself, both human and non-human, alike."

THE ULTIMATE ACTIVISM

"As the psychedelic experience heightens for each D-Xer, Ivanka further entices each MAN with her personalized AI mystical magic, brilliantly enacted by Louise. As each of them drop in deeper, they feel more fully the zero mental gravity created by the OM App, while viewing personalized inner-life scenarios perfectly choreographed for each Davosian and designed to relax heavily armored defense mechanisms, again, MDMA-like."

"By the way, Alan, I really like the way I'm feeling," Mr. Trump says with an broad unaffected smile. "Is this MDMA a company that trades publicly? Please give me the stock symbol a bit later, if you would. You're right, this is right up there with a hole in one times three. And far more interesting than being President. Just joking, of course."

"It's only going to get better, Sir. Let me continue, please. Soon each D-Xer arrives at total self-abandonment, while aroused by erotic images designed by one's own sublimated sexual fantasies.

"In other words, Elon has perfected a personalized AI sacred strip club in the OM chip, with the most exotic dancing by Louise, of course, super-imposed with "everything Ivanka." And as I said earlier, Mr. Trump, the OM technology offers a far better, more dimensional and intimate girlfriend experience than one's own wife or romantic partner.

"Stand forewarned, Sir, when the OM TANKA-X technology goes public, it will be the end of religion, and most likely childbirth too. So, we must be extremely careful who has access to it.

"But for now, we must stay true to mission – you, Donald J. Trump, returning to the Presidency and becoming the GREATEST SAVIOR – the ONE who saved the world from the death march of the global fascists, and in so doing, turned back the Doomsday Clock and preserved nature and life itself, for millennia to come.

"And I may add, you will also be the ONE who restores unity, peace and reconciliation for the people of America. As you know, Sir, there is no true winning without true healing, and that will only come when all the divisiveness in our country ceases, culminating with you and Joe playing a round of golf together. And soon, I hope. We may even consider a dual-presidency, alternating with three months on and three months off. But let's stay with PAYBACK FOR NOW."

"Yes, Alan. I'm OPEN. But keep it real for NOW. And please don't forget to give me the stock symbol for this MDMA – GREAT stuff. I may even BUY THE COMPANY and rename it MAGA. Sorry to interrupt. Please, carry on."

AN ANTI-PORN PARTY

"As each Davosian engages further in their OM generated personalized psychedelicized heart opening erotic sex show, OM simultaneously offers a guided meditation encouraging each D-Xer to become ONE with their feelings of LUST and not to be ashamed of this natural human emotion.

"OM continues, "Feel into your arousal and let the yearning for sexual union build. Be mindful of the warm sensations pulsing through your penis. Beautify your prick with a new language of intimacy and dignity. You have every right to embody your highest, most beautiful sexual WISDOM; sanctify the mystical gift of true tenderness and begin your journey of creating your own AWAKENED EMERGENCE into your divine feminine, the love of closeness, mutuality, and safety.

"OM's TANKA-X is the ultimate healing experience, Mr. Trump. A flawless transformational perfection, if you will. Integrating ONLY the finest wisdom of every female Saint, psychiatrist, artist, activist, indigenous elder, mother, writer, poet and spiritual teacher, that has ever lived throughout history.

"Elon even included the soul essence of such great women as Margaret Sanger, Maya Angelou, Audre Lorde, Betty Friedan, Gloria Steinem, Meyrl Streep, and his beloved girlfriend Grimes, along with such edgy luminaries, and some of my own favorites, Tricia Rose, Patti Smith, Maria Popova, Esther Perel, Margot Anand, Beyonce, Tracee Ellis Ross, Saint Vincent, Fatima Bhutto, Maggie VandenBerge, Amanda Palmer and V (formerly Eve Ensler).

"Elon was adamant about eliminating ALL toxic masculine energy from the "mindful intelligence conversion therapy" in order to achieve a 100% success rate, even among the most hardcore severely damaged neoliberal sociopathic corporate totalitarian deviants, as the Davosians and C.C.P. truly are.

"Over and over, we hear Ivanka's angelic spiritual-ly-inspired pure voice blend hypnotically with the voice of OM: "Become one with your desire to orgasm dear Man, and feel it as sacred, life giving, and healing."

"Meanwhile, as the sexual energy BUILDS, the conference hall echoes with a cacophony of dog howls and grunts of deviant undulating wealthy white miscreants yearning to cum.

"And as their animal-like nastiness loudens and the craving to orgasm heightens, OM instructs them with a strong but gentle voice to mindfully embrace their impulses with love and respect and to HOLD the URGE; "squeeze your sphincter muscle between your balls and your ass, UPWARD. HOLD IT. If you falter, bring your mindful COURAGE to that point of truth again and again and SQUEEZE in. HOLD IT.

"NOW, allow your desire to orgasm to fade, and as it does breathe in and feel the divine feminine energy caressing through every fiber of your sacred form. Allow the DF to heal you, cleanse you of all toxins and negative beliefs. Allow it to elevate your love of all Life, unconditionally and especially of nature, and of yourself as well. You are love. Feel it. Be it.

"Please do this again and again and again, SQUEEZE UP, beautiful man. And now breath into the God consciousness that pervades all life, and SQUEEZE up the Divine Feminine energy of radical self-acceptance – bring her high into your heart, and into your lungs and into every neuron of your brain. And now bring her down into the very DNA animating every cell of your entire Being, right now. Breathe into totality. Breathe into the Divine Feminine fully. BE ONE WITH THE SACRED."

"As Louise continues dancing Franceska-like as an AI created image of Ava-Ivanka in the face of each D-Xer, Elon, now enjoying his own orbit of Earth from his Space-X office, telepathically switches OM into hyperdrive, allowing each D-Xer to see Ava-Ivanka in a Hi-Def 4-D setting.

"Instantly, each D-Xer's environment is subconsciously self-generated and uniquely designed to intensify the next level of the Clockwork Orange-like TANKA-X "mindful intelligence conversion shock therapy." And thereby, fully excavate the rotten moral shit from the psyche of each Fourth Reichian.

"What they NOW see on their 360 degree 4-D mindscreens are their own family members. Each one of them are cruelly rounded up by demon-masked massive white men and stripped and beaten like animals. They are herded together and told to dive into a huge vat of "Magic Christian"-like putrefying maggot ridden animal excrement.

"They are told to wipe their faces with it, and to smell it and eat it. If they resist, they are whipped until they obey. "Eat more SHIT, you scum," the demons shout.

"This is how your husband treats us – the disenfranchised people of the world. You are low life. You steal our resources. You make us slave for you. You give weapons to our corrupt leaders. You pollute our lands with your poisons. You desecrate our lands with your imperialism. You are sociopaths in suits. Eat more SHIT. Smell it. Lick it. Your caucacity is as sickening as your INSANITY."

"We hear the porn mangled sounds of pre-orgasm as the 3,000 D-Xers undergoing the "conversion shock therapy" become paralyzed with REMORSE in their personalized OM-driven hell worlds.

"Meanwhile, they see an AI created image of the GODDESS dancing with her fully shaven dripping wet *Bodhisattva*-pussy in the hungry face of each D-Xer, forcing them to SPLIT OFF into two conflicting identities. Brilliantly produced by Elon, of course. On the one hand, they yearn to lick the GODDESS'S sacred *yoni* and on the other hand, are psychotically REPULSED by the denigration and humiliation of their wife and family.

"It is unbearable for them, Mr. Trump, to see their beloveds forced to eat shit and drink piss and blood and be shouted at and whipped because of their own lack of empathy and their sociopathic white privilege, provided for, no less, by their beloved Fourth Reichian husbands.

"None of this would have been needed, Sir, if only they had the ethical courage to address the election irregularities. Mathematics don't lie, and they were caught red handed. I bring this up because it points to how deep their pathology goes. They are determined to DESTROY you and the planet and all life with it, unless they are stopped."

"Soon, as the shock therapy continues to work its magic, each D-Xer is broken and shattered and as each man ungulates and wants to cum, OM reminds him of graphic images of how repulsive it is for his wife and family. Which forces him to want to purge, Ayahuasca-like. Over and again the oscillation of extremes occurs."

My inner *Mandala*'s Wheel of Life is now turning at its finest. My War on *Samsara* and my Journey of Wholeness must continue, I declare. I hear Bob in my ear, "Hit harder, Alan. Take EVIL down."

Once more addressing the President, I continue, "As the shock of conversion continues, each D-Xer feels his favorite music pumping through his brain and, laying outstretched in Elon's zero gravity reclining chair, they feel like they are going INSANE.

"In actuality, Mr. Trump, they did not realize they were already insane, and they are currently in transition to sanity. OM white privilege conversion SHOCK therapy, Sir, is most effective when administered with this new form of psychedelic that we gave each D-Xer. It's called "ETR-DMT" or "Existential Trauma Removing Dimethyltryptamine." This substance has been secretly produced and rarely used. This is the first mass test of its effectiveness. And it too will go public after you resume office, along with a complimentary 1,000,000 shares to you and a seat on the Board, should you wish."

ETR-DMT THERAPY

"As the "ETR-DMT conversion shock therapy" works its transformational magic, our D-Xers have no reference point to who and where they are. And with each intensifying minute, each man oscillates between the repulsion of physical torture and the torture of sexual lust. Each time they want to orgasm, it's ruined with the urge to purge.

"Again and again, each D-Xer spins in his individual *Samsara*, when, on the outer circumference of their 4-D mind-generated world of heaven and hell, a ring of fire – their mind's burning as it were – both symbolic of a human immolation and our earthly house on fire with imminent extinction.

"With every hour, each Fourth Reichian further abandons their identity until they enter a state of existential psychosis. Here time ceases and perspective is lost. Each man is now malleable enough to be un-brainwashed.

"If horror could get darker, a scenario that only the most advanced AI OM App could create, the images on their mind-screens are now of their wives being raped from the rear – "Game of Thrones"-like; one by one – by men wearing freaky Hitler masks.

"With each deep thrust, OM has lip-synced their

wives anguished groans to be the sounds of erotic pleasure. Their wives are heard saying, "I want more, Adolf. Do me harder. Go faster. Go deeper. Make me cum, Adolf."

"Simultaneously, our compassionate Franceska-like GODDESS has her sacred wet *yoni* in the face of each D-Xer. And again and again, each D-Xer begs the SACRED WOMAN to let him cum. And as he gets harder and his prick pulsates more intensely, and is about to shoot off, each Fourth Reichian is repulsed by his own LUST and sickened by the LIFE-LIKE images of his wife being sodomized, and loving it.

"Mr. Trump, the proclivity for EVIL goes deep, that we know. I, like you, wish such men would voluntarily change their aberrant ways, but the human brain isn't wired that way at this time in evolution. I know this conversion shock therapy is severe, but since religion doesn't work and nothing ever gets done in the Washington Swamp, ETR-DMT therapy is the only way to STOP THE DOOMSDAY CLOCK. The future of life is at stake. And none of us want to give up hope on a sustainable future. We pray this therapy does the job. And moreover, you return to the helm of the world."

"I fully understand the compassion behind the vision, Alan," Mr. Trump explains.

"Over and over," I continue, "the D-Xers psychotically oscillate between their primordial lust to orgasm with the GODDESS' WAP in their face, and hellishly repulsed by the masked Hitler men thrusting themselves into their wives from the rear and loving it. The D-Xers yell out, "STOP. Please STOP. No, more. No. Don't stop. MORE, I want to cum. Let me cum. Please let me cum. No. NO. Stop, more, more. NO, more, please. No. No. Stop. Please STOP."

"Next, each Fourth Reichian's family, and their colleagues, too, are seen in a Yemen-like dystopian setting, smoldering with fires and charred landscapes of bombed out buildings in ruins. Thousands of propaganda pamphlets with bright red, white and blue US flags festooned with Bush-Cheney-Obama-Biden faces are blowing in the torrid dusty wind.

"We see large flat screens on poles protruding Big Brother-like from the ruins, and from the black and white static appears highly pixelated live images of Joe Biden reading from a teleprompter from his basement with his mask off, stating, "Now that I am President, I will EXPAND America's FOREVER WARS. Just as I did in calling for the invasion of Iraq and Afghanistan, IT is my solemn duty as a Democratic US President to uphold my promise to you – the American people – to protect justice, peace and universal rights wherever needed, REGARDLESS OF THE HORROR IT CREATES FOR OTHERS.

"Further, as my record clearly shows, I DEMANDED that we give to our beloved Saudi-women hating Brothers as many hi-tech weapons as desired, in order to maim and KILL as many of those worthless vermin in Yemen as possible. And I DO NOT GIVE A FUCK if it created the greatest humanitarian disaster this century. That is a small price to pay to increase the profits of our corporate sponsors and keep my fellow American's happy.

"Meanwhile, scum bag Donald J. is an idiot psychopathic PIG who made friends with America's greatest enemy, Kim Jong-un. He and Trump are the twin pillars of EVIL in our world and they must ERASED."

"The OM software instantly switches channels from Biden and detects each D-Xer's greatest fear. OM instantly translates that projected FEAR into the behaviors of wife and family and friends on their inner screens.

"Family members are now seen foraging the earth for food and water and crying and bleeding and starving in their disorientation. Each family member displays the most severe symptoms of Human Devastation Syndrome, the most monstrous expression of PTSD ever known on Earth.

"And now our AI generated GODDESS asks each D-Xer, "Do you want to lick me just one time? Are you ready for me? Will you give anything I want to lick my wet ass pussy? Will you be my boy toy?"

"And each Fourth Reichian says in Big Brother uniformity, "Yes, anything Ava. We will do anything." And she asks again, "Anything?"

"Yes, anything Goddess Ava," they reply, as if one voice is speaking in Big Brother-like harmony. Anything to stop the horror to my wife, family and friends.

"Instantly, the circumstances are reversed. Now,

each Fourth Reichian sees himself in his mind's eye as the refugee – naked, starving and traumatized.

"They cannot tell it is a projection of their own sublimated fear, Mr. Trump. The AI Team is unparalleled in perfecting the hallucination in full 4-D reality, and the sensation of purging by the meta-intelligence inherent in the ETR-DMT molecule.

"The OM Goddess is heard asking each D-Xer again, with a boundless heart of compassion, "Anything?"

"Yes," they reply in unison. "Free me of this HORROR, please." Meanwhile, the scenario is sound tracked to each man's favorite music. The cleansing of their dissociated dominator insanity goes even deeper.

"The GODDESS asks them, "Do you realize you created this situation that you are now in? Do you realize that you are the one who wholesales this neocolonialist, nature destroying, life subjugating, dehumanizing sickness around the world? Do you understand? All for money. Your fetish for profit. Your addiction to violence. Your own narcissism. Do you understand your own EVIL?"

"We so understand, Goddess Ava," they ALL say in a uniform voice of REVERENTIAL worship. "We promise we will never do anything to harm anyone ever again. "Never. We promise."

"As each man remains paralyzed and suspended painlessly in OM's zero gravity, each D-Xer breaks down fully inside their own mind and begins to whimper and

WEEP, saying softly through their tears, "I'm sorry for my greed. It's unconscionable what I have done. How foolish I have been."

"Next each D-Xer sees an emaciated seven year-old child a few days before starving to death. The skin draped skeleton makes eye contact with the D-Xer, and says, 'You may have read this in the New York Times but here it is for real. This is what your weapons have done. Look at me. I have no parents. I have not eaten in forty-five days. Starvation is insanely cruel and terrifying. I cannot control my bowels. My skin is peeling off. My hair is gone. I hallucinate nightmarish images day and night. I'm almost blind. I am cannibalizing myself. I am eating myself from the inside out; my own muscles and organs and even my heart. I sleep on the earth like a rat. I have stopped crying. I am this way because of you. And soon, this will be your future as well. You will be forced into cannibalism. The collapse will have no mercy on you or anyone else around the world. All for profit.'

"Each D-Xer weeps louder than ever before.

"Mr. Trump, to conclude 'the ETR-DMT assisted, mindful conversion shock session,' OM administers a high dose of odorless vaporized Ayahuasca and each D-Xer has a full plant medicine experience. Each D-Xer is made to feel as if they are purging over and over again, but it too is an illusion from OM. The feeling of the experience however is real.

"As each D-Xer purges his DNA-drenched toxic cruel

tendencies, he sees vivid symbols of his own evil spilling out of his mouth: a rapid set of graphic images and circumstances associated with the HELL he has created on Earth. This is called anti-trauma porn, Mr. Trump. The opposite of "Game of Thrones."

"And slowly, with each purge, they begin to feel themselves as inseparable from all life. Each one in the room cries out for MERCY TO BE FOREGIVEN for his own blind delusion. Each one in the room screams out, "NEVER AGAIN. I WILL BE HUMAN. A harmless loving human being."

"Our beloved GODDESS of COMPASSION asks with the HEART of a *Buddha*-to-be, "And you voluntarily wish to give your entire wealth to my FATHER – DONALD J. TRUMP – for him to do what you failed to do, which is to Save America and the World too?"

"Yes, we promise. We trust you FULLY, Goddess Ava, and we trust your Father. You have restored our sight, when we were blind. We are forever devoted to you and your beloved Father too."

"Wonderful," she says with a tone of honor. "OM has recorded your voice print agreement."

"Each D-Xer is then given an OM induced inhalant anesthesia and each man quietly goes into deep sleep.

"After they sleep like babies for the night, Mr. Trump, they are transformed, completely. They have been cleansed of Evil and replaced with a heroic level of the Divine Feminine. MISSION ACCOMPLISHED.

"Each member of the global elite assume that what happened occurred in a dream.

"Thus, Mr. Trump, that is just a taste of Davos-X. That is the opening session. From that point on, you take over and inflict maximum payback for their stealing of the election, as you prepare for your imminent return to the White House.

"And as an added bonus, Sir, the next time any of the D-Xers see you, including their families and associates, they think of you as a modern-day Gandhi. After all you are. They also see you as the inspiration to have stopped the Doomsday Clock and the car from hitting the brick wall of human generated extinction.

"They subsequently call off their interest in the Green New Deal and pledge allegiance to your climate policy, which is a mandatory worldwide use of the next iteration of OM – a vaccine that administers a personalized one hour only experience of "ETR-DMT assisted transformational self-hatred therapy," offered freely, except to the C.C.P., of course. They get a weaponized version that miraculously turns communist men towards Buddhism.

"You, Sir, have successfully become the greatest human that ever lived. The metaphysical Rocky who saved the world from the sixth mass extinction. And yes, you will indeed win the Nobel Peace Prize, as will Ava-Ivanka, of course."

"Wow, amazing Alan. By the way, I really, really like

this MDMA stuff. I should start offering it to my staff at Mar-a-Lago and at my hotels as well. Frankly, once I own the company, I'll give a years' supply as a peace offering both to the Pentagon and Congress. I'll even ask Joe if he wants to host a joint MDMA HEALING OF THE POLITICAL DIVIDE PARTY at the White House. We can televise it as the "White House of Rocky" and show the American people the power of love and reconciliation. Anyway, I love Davos-X. It works. Let's do it."

REUNION WITH MYSELF

Back in the House of Rocky, I picked up the morphine, imagining what awaited me on the other side. After reflecting on Bob's passionate plea to "NEVER GIVE UP," I summoned the courage to KEEP engaging my own War with *Samara* and challenge the forces of evil swirling through my own heart and mind.

As I had done thousands of times before, I adjusted my bodily posture to one of a composed cross-legged meditating yogi. Found my balance, sitting upright, with hands folded on my lap. I relaxed my breath and allowed it to sink into the lower abdomen and from there to breathe on its own in uncontrolled rhythms of naturalness. As I gently closed my eyes, interior space was illuminated.

While mindful of the pulsing of my heart, I sent a deliberate determination to the primordial origins of MY

BEING: "THE LAST STAND. Let the highest *Dharma* that I need to know at this time be revealed in order to STAY ALIVE, FIGHT ON, and take actions for a better world."

Within minutes, I was enveloped by a holographic memory of unconditional love. And as I felt into its radiance, the face of my beloved therapist Shakti-Ma appeared as pure Divine Feminine light. As I let her into my heart, I felt a strong psychic pull to speak with her.

Navigating the peak state of the psychedelic, I found her number on my iPhone. Pressing each digit mindfully – one by one – as if touching the skin of an angel from afar; I heard the ringing of her phone, as if meditating to the sound of the chimes as I had done hundreds of times before inside Notre Dame.

Seven, eight, nine rings ... and just as I was to press END, she picked up. And within minutes we were on Zoom together, connecting for the first time in over twenty years. And we picked up right where we left off – not only as lovers in her home-office, as only her clients were allowed to do – but also as soul allies reuniting with our long history of transparency, tears and laughter. Along with her foremost requirement – a dedication to truth-telling, regardless of the consequences.

As we spoke, I became more mindful of the magic we once shared. The effortless flow of eroticized *Ubuntu* – the synergy of high energy, emotions, and CREATIVE ideas. And as we reimagined sacred space together, we remembered the rarity of our sapiosexual chemistry, and felt it re-arise, even stronger than before.

Too bad she was my therapist, I thought. But blessed that she brought me back to life, post monasticism.

And now, she was 75 and her black hair was fully silver and her Eurasian smooth face – once a beauty – was deeply creased from age and years of unprotected sunlight. And as if reading my mind, she quipped: "Just think, movie stars used to pay me $1000 an hour to fly on their private jets to exotic hideaways. Now, even the most senior spiritual teachers, some of them pushing 65, 70 and even 80, would rather book my 20-something Bali trained tantra gals, rather than me – the Grand Madame of Marin County, and the Holiest of places.

"Ironically," she continued with a satirical tone, "it's the under 50-year-old new batch of "online trained mindfulness teachers" that seek me out, and the rare bi-women as well. They much prefer to heal over Zoom than in flesh."

"Regardless, men never cease to surprise me" she carried on with a laugh, "with their willingness to sell their souls for good-looking pussy and profit, especially those spiritually awakened men.

"What's new, right? Now what about you? Tell me you've stopped pretending, Alan," she stated with a loving smile.

Seconds later when we stopped laughing, she

engaged me in a long silence of eye to eye and heart to heart, pouring out our genuine love for each other. I then told her I was on a high dose of acid. To which she cutely quipped, "I was wondering how you were able to be so sincere."

After another great laugh, I explained that I had just arrived from a military-controlled Burma – my final trip after nearly fifty years – and I'm here in Santa Monica at my dear friend's home – Bob Chartoff – who had passed away a few years ago.

I went onto explain how I had chosen this very day to find a reason to stay alive, and if I could not find an answer, mindfully take my life. I held up the morphine and told her I was prepared to inject it before midnight, if I had not, in fact, genuinely found hope to face societal collapse and near term human extinction.

Shakti-Ma got serious and said in a caring voice, "I so get it, Alan. I too struggle with why to stay alive. And I will not try to talk you out of not taking your life. Although I assume you've reached out today not to say hello and goodbye after twenty-two years, but to process your heart space, clear your conscience, let go of the past, explore if there is anything left undone. What is it? How can I support you?

"Before you answer, let me say this. From the acid, the horrors in Burma, and everything else you are dealing with, you are in a heightened state of sensitivity. Let me first guide you in cleansing your past of all negative configurations, and if there is still something to address at the end, I'm here, fully."

After re-engaging soul space, she spoke with me as only a Goddess of love and wisdom could. "Alan, whatever you decide to do tonight, do it with a clear and mindful heart. As for now, let go, relax and release every hurt, every fear, every judgment, and every betrayal you have ever made or had done towards you. It is easy to end the war and turn it around in a radiant expression of selflove. Make the noble choice, here at this existential crossroad. Drop the weight, Alan, fully. Don't carry it into the future. Open the heart. Release every negative association.

"Release those frauds tripping on turpitude who played and betrayed you for their own gain. They sleep in depravity and will reap what they sow. Release those who undermined your career with their backbiting and slander. Man up. Release those who have spoken ill of you and created controversies about you. Their hypocrisy is not yours to correct. As your teacher said to you, "let them fry in their own oil."

"Let go of the pain of past lovers. They did what they did because of their own uncharted trauma and fear. And the same with the pain you caused some of them. You can free yourself right now, fully, Alan. Release. Allow. Let go.

"Again, let go of everyone who may have hurt you, or you them. See them in your mind's eye and wish them well. See them as *dharma* brothers and sisters along this long journey of life. We all lie. We are all frauds. We are all hypocrites. We are all scammers and cheats. That's nature.

"What makes us different is that we see it in ourselves and embrace it, and in so doing, release ourselves from the prison of righteousness and self-deception.

"Now, I want you to breathe with me and let us look into each other's eyes. I want us to breath slowly and in harmony with each other and let our magic create a force of purity and beauty and transformation. We are light, Alan. Let this light dispel darkness in all directions, inside and outside.

"Let us sit here now and slowly breath together, Alan, and let the LIGHT of the DHARMA heal everything we have ever done in our lives to harm others, knowingly or unknowingly.

"I love you, Alan. And I know you love me. I am here with you and for us, together in life and in death. In breath, slowly dissolve. Out breath, feel it throughout our entire body. Release and BE."

Throughout the hour of silence, I mindfully released every fiber of discernible negative history; every hurt, every pain, every fear and betrayal.

I then brought into clear focus the mind and heart and face of each lover, each dear friend, each major teacher, guide and supporter, and my beloved daughter and her

Mother. I enveloped each of them with unconditional love.

And then I was back with my eyes wide open with my beloved Shakti-Ma. We smiled and said goodbye and then closed our eyes together in prayer. I was sure it was for the final time we would speak again in this life.

BURNING IN HEAVEN

As I opened my eyes in the House of Rocky, the acid expanded my awareness to a larger sphere of inclusivity. With old skins shedding, a prism of new identities emerged, casting themselves in full clarity on the cave walls of my own consciousness.

Like Aristotle's dance of projected self-shadows, I was at first enchanted by their novelty, until I saw through their nature and turned to face the light. And with it a virgin landscape alive with hyper-dimensional deities, enthralled with their celestial pleasures and transcendental toys.

For a moment, I craved an escape from our earthly horrors, to engage with them in their mystical orgies – merging transparent bodies of multi-colored light with waves of oceanic orgasms, that never seemed to end.

Time stopped, as did the Doomsday Clock, and I momentarily bathed in the stunning suddenness of my psychedelic-assisted new dimension of intra-Being. Awed, as it were, by the deities' limitless visions of co-creative splendor and mind games of hyper-transcendental bliss.

"Look more closely, Alan," came the calm, clear voice of my late Burmese *Dhamma* teacher, Sayadaw U Pandita. "Ask yourself, what do you see?"

"I see the flames of impermanence, Sir."

"Exactly," he replied. "Subtle as it is, every realm burns with ignorance. Here, too, there's a Doomsday Clock. But these deities are too entranced with lust to see the ephemeral fabric of their own existence. Turn away, Alan. Just as you did in Aristotle's cave. Face the light of reality, not the shadow of projection. Affirm your commitment to truth and freedom and carry on."

I encouraged myself, saying, 'I want to know the meaning of hope in the face of imminent societal collapse and with it, WHY stay alive to co-exist with the horrors of mass starvation, perpetual disease and WAR – endless murder. Why stay alive? Why?'

I hear the hypnotic voices of Buddhist monks chanting *Buddham saranam gacchami* over and over again. Along with the words of Sayadaw U Pandita, "Alan, never give up, RISE UP, find hope where there is none. Take refuge in the *Buddha*. Not the man, but the experience of AWAKENING to your highest, most liberated frequency. Breathe."

"Embody your BEST, Alan." I hear you Bob, loud and clear.

Dhammam saranam gacchami. "Take refuge in the *Dhamma*. Dedicate yourself, Alan, to discovering your

Notre Dame, your own Divine Feminine – and the time-less laws and lessons needed to escape this *Samsaric* house on fire."

Sangham saranam gacchami. "Take refuge in the *Sangha*, Alan. Take refuge in the most liberated minds that have ever lived and BRING THEM together in a final mystical BATTLE to win your War with *Samsara*."

I hear Rocky talking to me: "Let me tell you some-thing you already know, Alan. The world ain't all sunshine and rainbows. It's a mean and nasty place and I don't care how tough you are it will beat you to your knees and keep you there permanently, if you let it.

"You, me, or nobody is gonna hit as hard as life. But it ain't about how hard ya hit, Alan. It's about how hard you can get hit and keep moving forward. How much you can take and keep up the fight. That's how winning is done, Alan! So win it. Perseverance is everything."

THE CLOCK IS MOVED FORWARD

Realizing the catastrophic implications of America's Kafkaesque landscape and the EXISTENTIAL EMERGENCY with the ONSLAUGHT of GLOBAL TOTALITARIANISM and LIKELIHOOD of NUCLEAR WAR, Chicago's atomic scientists decided to UNANIMOUSLY move the Doomsday Clock forward from 100 seconds, to 10 seconds before midnight.

Every psychiatrist knows that when you take the

world's most powerful narcissist and have his nemesis – the C.C.P.-Democratic One World Totalitarian Party – who spent billions in ads comparing him to Hitler, it only stands, one would not only seek PAYBACK, but evoke GLOBAL JIHAD itself.

Surprisingly, no one saw this coming, and averted TRUMP'S REVENGE by simply supporting an impartial investigation of his claims of "election fraud." For no other reason than to support the integrity of the democratic process, the conscience of the American Constitution, and the essential freedoms of the greatest Republic in the history of Earth.

But NO, none of the criminal elite wanted to give Donald J. a second term, no matter what. Yet, if they had only done what was fair and just, WHAT WAS BEST FOR THE COUNTRY and THE VERY FUTURE OF FREEDOM ITSELF, WE THE PEOPLE would have been spared FULL MELTDOWN. The primacy of profit was simply too inbuilt to see clearly. And hatred festered into blindness.

On the other side of spectrum, I kick myself in the ass for not being more ADAMANT with the President. If ONLY he had listened to me when he called. I explained in no uncertain terms that I had psychic-intuitive-INTEL indicating there would be BIG trouble on the day of his infamous speech on January 6, 2021.

"Sir, you MUST BE UNAMBIGUOUS in telling your followers to not only peacefully march to the U.S. Capital, BUT TO NOT ENTER IT. Rather, quietly surround the sacred site and SIT DOWN IN MEDITATIVE SILENCE.

"Further," I explained, "You, Sir, were responsible for introducing mindfulness to our combat troops overseas. It happened under your watch. To "kill" without regret. To "kill" without stress. To "kill" in good conscience. You must walk your "mindful" talk, Sir.

"Please bring that powerful mental tool to your MAGA followers. HAVE THEM SIT DOWN IN SILENCE at the Capital and send mindful waves of loving kindness to our lawmakers; support them in the grueling electoral process; show the world the conscious and caring man that YOU are."

NO. Not even with my forty years of service in the Agency would he listen. All it would have taken was for him to include a few additional sentences in his speech, and America would have been truly REBORN.

IF ONLY he could hear me: "Embrace your inner Gandhi, Sir; please, Mr. President, for the future of our Great Country – for establishing "mindful democracy" in America and around the world. Have everyone sit in loving meditative silence for twenty minutes and then have them go home, quietly and reverentially, as if leaving Church."

After striking the iceberg, the Titanic sunk in 2 hours and 40 minutes. And the same with America. Such is the nature of our own limitations and with it, the sinking of a country and the drowning of Empire.

History is history. Welcome to the Apocalypse.

TRUMP'S REVENGE

I can hear Trump in his Rocky-like thunder, scream, "DON'T BET AGAINST ME! I'll show them!"

My new mission: I hereby commit to a personal crusade known as DONALD J. TRUMP'S REVENGE.

ONE wonders if this was preplanned. Was TRUMP really a closet Jihadist in disguise? The self-fulfilling prophecy of a billionaire suicide bomber with the world's largest supply of nuclear weapons at his disposal?

Is this real or is it another Davos-X like hallucination, I wondered?

We know that Trump has the full support of the Pentagon hierarchy. Many of those Generals are as OUTRAGED as he. They are also inspired by the Rapture-entranced, China-hating, former Secretary of State, Michael Pompeo.

These men own the military. They own the NUKES. They own the "nuclear football," the 45-pound suitcase the President carries with him everywhere, that contains the nuclear codes. And a hacked set of those same codes, by a former President as well. These men own the nuclear subs. They own the mind set of conquering evil. And these men mainline evangelical crack and could easily rain Armageddon on the masses and accelerate their assent into eternal life in Heaven.

As a rush of URGENCY swept up my spine, I remembered the Vietnamese monk's immolation in my dream.

"Hope for the best, prepare for the worse," Aung San Suu Kyi's words echoed, cracking the monk's image within my mind. "Those are my father's thoughts," she told me. "He was assassinated days later." And she was rearrested by the military dictator not long after telling me her father's dictum.

Don't underestimate the power of S.H.I.T., Alan. What's the worst that can happen, I reflected? What's the hardest punch that S.H.I.T could throw? Embrace your greatest fear and hope for the best. My inner *Mandala* took on new meaning.

DYSTOPIA IMAGINED

If TRUMP, now in his Mar-a-Lago fortress, with his DEEP STATE allies and Pentagon diehards, were to enact Rapture-inspired REVENGE, what might it look like?

I closed my eyes and saw a blinding light as I entered Mr. Trump's psyche and the darkened folds of his repressed shadow.

First out, it's PAYBACK with a precision guided digital assault that drains the bank accounts and stock portfolios of the 80 million sheeple who hated Trump enough to vote for Beijing Biden and the fascist Left, along with every sell-out Republican who abandoned the President at the most critical moment in American history.

Next out, Dictator Xi Jinping of China and the 90 million cyborgs of his genocidal Communist Chinese

Party are infected with a weaponized-pork-precision "Gandhian bio-virus" that renders each of them nonviolent vegan pacifists, and with it goes the entire gene pool that ordered the ethnic cleansing of the Uyghur's, the persecution of Tibetans, and the wholesale imprisonment of freedom fighters in Hong Kong.

In a goodbye salute to Oligarchy, Amazon's headquarters in Seattle was spared and given to the employees to run as a collective. While CEO Jeff Bozos and his new honey are sent into exile in Bali, and after a training in trauma-release breathwork and Neo-*Tantra* sexual union, given a mansion on the side of Mount Agung in a secretive healing community, frequented by such notables as Brazil's President Bolsonaro, Charlie Rose, George Pell, Sogyal Rinpoche, and Jeffrey Epstein, and owned and operated by "the icon of spiritual healing," Russel Simmons.

At the behest of Trump's high-five Brother Kim Jong-un, Mitch McConnell and Nancy Pelosi, along with both the House and Senate Democrats, and the back-stabbing Republicans, plus a few others from Georgia, along with Liz Cheney, are sent to North Korea.

Apparently, Kim asked that America's most elite globalist think tank advise him on how to transition from dictatorship to democracy. Sadly, however, the Swamp was housed in squalled quarters on the outskirts of Pyongyang, that slowly turned into "Animal Farm," with some pigs becoming more equal than others, despite doing their jobs well.

President Biden and his gifted son Hunter were sadly given to Steven K. Bannon, where they both underwent a second round of "ETR-DMT assisted mindful conversion shock therapy," to further purge them of their neoliberal fascist indoctrination.

Once completed, Joe joyously juggled his time from the White House with that of joining Steve and Raheem as co-hosts on their daily talk show, "War Room Pandemic" that was renamed, "We Stopped the Doomsday Clock."

Hunter, on the other hand, after the mega-success of his best selling memoir, "Beautiful Things: From My Hard Drive from Hell to Heaven in the White House with the Man," needed a third round of "conversion therapy," that, according to Elon, unfortunately, still didn't work. So the cycle will continue every week, according to a press release, until it does work. Oddly, word had it that he liked "therapy" so much he did not want it to stop.

DYSTOPIA CONTINUES
CHINA GETS WOKE

The New York Times, Washington Post, CNN, MSNBC, and FOX, and dozens of other smaller media outlets, were liquidated to Miles Guo, the exiled Chinese billionaire, who compassionately took the helm and returned them to truly democratic voices for the freedom loving people of the world.

Apparently, all former employees working for these media titans begged Miles to keep them on, saying they were perfunctorily manipulated to produce and publish deliberate lies and misinformation under their former bosses. Miles assured them that "respect for universal human rights, especially freedom of thought and speech, is all that matters under his leadership," and not only kept them working, he gave them huge pay raises and shares in the company.

Even former Dictator Xi Jinping invited Miles to return to China to assist him in "taking down the C.C.P., as well as the firewall within the minds of the people." In so doing, Gandhi-Xi-gyi, his newly adopted name, begged Miles to "establish freedom of expression in our beloved Motherland with respect to timeless spiritual values."

Miles respectfully declined, recommending that Xi-gyi – demonstrate the power of his conversion –by incinerating the three trillion images of himself through-out the country. Then assist his 90 million C.C.P. members in undergoing "ETR-DMT assisted mindful conversion shock therapy," and once done, demonstrate its effec-tiveness by returning Tibet to the Dalai Lama and the Tibetan people, while paying them five trillion dollars in restitution.

In addition, releasing the three million Uyghur

Muslims from concentration camps, and giving each person one million dollars. Still further, releasing all Hong Kong pro-democracy activists and not only returning Hong Kong to the people, but apologizing to them and to the world for the harm caused. Xi-gyi also agreed to Mile's final request: that of making Taipei the new capital of China.

Although Miles never did return to his native country, preferring to stay close to his new media enterprises and his penthouse in Manhattan, Xi-gyi and Miles were often seen having (vegan only) dinners at Masa at the Time Warner Building, also now owned by Miles.

Still further, after Xi-gyi admitted on CNN that the Wuhan Bio-Virus was indeed weaponized, the world over celebrated how enemies could truly become friends. And Miles was the first to make "RECONCILIATION" a recurring headline, especially in his newly formed "New York Anti-fascist China Times" newspaper, freely offered, worldwide.

DYSTOPIA CONTINUES
AMERICA BECOMES GREAT

As Trump's revenge gathers momentum, even true-blue American Democrats started to actively seek MAGA lovers to show their devotion to God and national healing.

Not unexpectedly, should 'hard-to-break-a-habit-Joe' relapse, a rare Supreme Court ruling granted Mr. Bannon the right to engage the President in a series of "anti-struggle self-love sessions" – with the assistance of Dr. Jill – Joe's wife, of course – to help him understand, at the most visceral level, the value of honesty, basic human decency, genuine generosity and warmth, the plight of the working class, and the true meaning of freedom and democracy.

The ruling also made it mandatory for any American protesting the fall of the neoliberal totalitarian agenda to undergo "mandatory mental vaccination" – a three-second visual poke of "ETR-DMT mindful-conversion shock therapy" that purges one of their "Trump Derangement America Last Disorder," once and for all.

To make America really great this time, Mr Trump, inspired by Mahatma Gandhi's famous "stop work order" that paralyzed the white imperialist economy of India back in the '40s, took it much further, and ordered the FED to print money year-round. Thus, giving free cash to everyone, in perpetuity, to NO LONGER WORK.

This new, "Anti-Stimulus Year Around Care to Pursue Your Dreams Policy" was a hit among everyone, especially drug addicts, illegal aliens, inner city homeless, and wayward teenagers who flooded the streets and Spotify with the most innovative RAD music, and the greatest Tik Tok dance videos ever seen.

Overall, the working class, finally free of serfdom, renewed ties with their families and friends, developing much deeper bonds within community, and even returned to church on a regular basis. Caring for one other swept the country, far faster than Covid, panic porn, and mandatory vaccinations, back in the day.

Soon, even the Democratic strong holds throughout the States, formerly zones of arson, looting and terror, became festival-like, even reverential at times, with mass public prayer groups and the singing of holy hymns throughout the night.

Even Antifa, choosing to remove their black SS-like uniforms and wear festive Burning Man-like costumes, laid down their hatred through the generous volunteer support of *yoga* teachers and mindfulness coaches, who no longer needed to work online, as the virus miraculously disappeared as the fear and insecurity evaporated from the lives of both Americans and citizens worldwide.

Finally, the slogan "Black Lives Mattered" was replaced with "It All Started With Us," and within the Lincoln Memorial a second seat was created with a statue of George Floyd.

Further, the Supreme Court unanimously agreed that Brother Floyd be granted the honor as a Founding Father. In so doing, they ordered that his infamous image of "I Can't Breathe" be painted on all images alongside Jefferson, Washington and Adams.

The White House itself was transformed and painted like a zebra.

DYSTOPIA CONTINUES
A NEW ERA OF HOPE

In this new era of hope, the infamous Wall along America's notorious border with Mexico was quickly dismantled and everyone who wanted to escape their tragic lives as robbers, rapists and drug dealers were given life-long US passports, rent free homes in Death Valley, and unlimited bank cards.

They especially felt honored to support Trump's "Make the World Great Again" Campaign, and did everything possible to confine their 'hard to break criminal habits' to members of their own community. Eventually, Mitt Romney and George Bush converted them to respectful members under the Lord's guidance and Death Valley became a fertile oasis of love, religion, and prosperity.

The only downside, despite Covid disappearing, was that due to the success of "The Great Davos Green-Globalization ReSet Campaign," the world's 440 nuclear power plants melted down, creating the Chernobylization of much of the planet. As a result, those annoying Covid masks that now covered every ocean surface and beach worldwide, were replaced with SGE 400 Nuclear Full Head Coverings. Fortunately, however, they were outfitted with Bose speakers and new miniature iPhones.

Since Apple no longer needed to use slave labor in China to build their wares, and had no wages to pay employees due to the FEDs "CASH FOR ALL FOREVER

PLAN," they converted the company to a non-profit 501 3 c and gave free iPhones and MacBooks to all, and free service as well.

Apple even restored the Parler Social Media App to their iPhones after Jeff Bezos, from his home in Bali, asked his former company to please restore Parler's cloud services, while offering a full apology to the people of America for his unmindful denigration of free speech. An Amazon press release soon followed explaining that the services had already been restored, along with providing Parler free cloud services forever, in addition to giving them 10,000 of Amazon's finest technicians.

Bernie Sanders was so impressed with the epic evolution of his revolution he ceased his preoccupation with socialism and became a student of Trump's anti-capitalist utopia-ism crusade that was being crowdfunded by a new wave of anti-imperialist millennial philanthropists, dedicated to giving away all their inherited blood money to all inhabitants of 3rd and 4th world countries, especially ones devastated by American weapons and unbridled expansionism.

In this new era of hope, restaurants, bars, cinemas, museums, arenas, theaters, stadiums and night clubs all re-opened and also offered their services freely. Ironically, meditation centers and *yoga* studios became relics of the past, because no "teachers" wanted to teach without charging a fee for their teachings.

Big concerts even restarted, but sadly, U2 was the only group that went bankrupt during the pandemic. As such, they pleaded with First Nation Tour Company, as well as their audience, that they needed to charge for their shows in order to return to solvency.

Sadly, few came out to see them.

But true to their commitment to artistry and activism, they played to near vacant stadiums around the world, as few dared to "pay" and brave the trauma of being in such isolated environments while surrounded by thousands of uniformed defunded aggressive armed guards, holding back angry hungry German Shepherds as well.

Bono's long-time friend, Sir Bob Geldof, was quoted in Rupert Murdoch's infamous tell-all-tattler, "The Sun," that he figured U2's failure to draw arena-sized crowds, as before, was not due to charging for tickets. After all, he reminded them, they were the highest grossing act pre-Covid with sold out shows worldwide and with tickets up to $3k each. The fault was found with Bono's "cowardly recanting of his call for Aung San Suu Kyi, Burma's Noble Peace laureate, to resign for her evil complicity with the ethnic cleansing of the Rohingya Muslims" in her country.

In so doing, Geldof felt shamed by Bono and his own life-risking, on the ground, Pulitzer Prize winning investigative journalism in Burma, that discovered first-hand that Suu Kyi was in fact a sold out "handmaiden of genocide," as he told the world when he gave back his "Freedom of Dublin Award", to protest her DENIED obsession with military dictatorship, mass subjugation, and ethnic cleansing.

Some things have a way of coming back to bite you. Geldof, sadly, contracted Covid-19 from his pet mink, but did not die, despite losing smell and cognitive acuity.

Overall, there were headlines worldwide and celebrations in nearly every city, of how the SAVIOR DONALD J. TRUMP freed the world of the EVIL-TOTALITARIAN GLOBALISTS and ended their libertarian mandate of eternal stay at home lockdowns, mandatory vaccinations and no porn during the evening news.

The final issue of the Times before Miles took over, recanted their unrelenting vilification of Mr. Trump and apologized in a headline: "How We Foolish Got It Wrong – Donald J. Trump and His New Age of Moral Decency and Global Prosperity."

No one really cared that the electrical grid had gone down in most places worldwide, and fires consumed forests almost everywhere. And so what that Australia burned to the ground, other than Byron Bay, which survived unscathed due to a protective spiritual dome that was constructed around the region by a month-long Kirtan chanting festival, funded, no less, by the spiritual movie-star influencer federation of the world.

Although food supplies had been disrupted, the new employee-run Amazon Coop-Prime delivered any item desired by anyone in the world overnight, and both the item and delivery were offered freely.

Malware, unfortunately, hit the internet, except in Russia, Ukraine, and Washington D.C., and all but our Kindles, Androids, iPhones and crypto-wallets were erased.

Google miraculous stayed afloat, transitioning to a solar powered version of itself, called Google Light. But without email. Oddly, the world roared with delight and the very sound of the word "email" made people nauseous.

Handwritten letters became the new sexy and postal workers were allowed to dress any way they wanted. Some were even seen to be topless. And without the need for money, many of these selfless workers doubled as door-to-door sex therapists and voter integrity coaches.

Facebook became egalitarian and was renamed All-One-Face, with all selfies banned, including Donald Trump.

Zuckerberg on the other hand, Trump's Doctor Phil, was compassionately spared and re-positioned as the Zoom-based Warden of San Quentin from his 700-acre palatial estate on Kauai. There – at Cyborg Mansion – all Tech CEOs and their board of directors and top shareholders were permanently quarantined, to contain the new, more lethal "Extreme-Greed-2021 Virus." Whereas those among them who could not overcome the virus and were caught trying to do something for profit and/or watching porn, where actually sent to San Quentin for a three-month intensive "mind cleansing" of eight hours of daily *yoga*, fasting, meditation, colonics, and of course, "ETR-DMT assisted mindful conversion psychedelic shock therapy for obsessive-compulsive GREED vultures."

Jack Dorsey of Twitter was also fortunate enough to gain Mr. Trump's compassion and was offered a plea bargain to be exiled to Myanmar, where he could meditate in peace and teach mindfulness to the dictator and other military generals for the rest of his life. Of course, Trump agreed and took over Twitter and gave it to Steve Bannon to oversee.

Dorsey beautifully thanked Trump in an open letter in Mile's New York Anti-Fascist China Times, for "Giving me back my life. I had no idea how lost I had become with my billions. I was blinded by delusion. Now I can see again, thanks to the power of mindfulness, and to you, Sir, I offer a deep bow of gratitude. Keep at it my friend. I'm all in on the "Mindful MAGA Movement from Military Dictatorship Controlled Myanmar.""

Teams of highly trained mindfulness teachers descended into the new ghettos of America and successfully reduced the stress of the disenfranchised living in Beverley Hills, Westchester Country, the Hampton's, Silicon Valley, Palm Beach and other such elitist strong holds of those who refused to take permanent handouts from the government.

Plant medicine clinics replaced pharmacies, finally, and teams of Peruvian trained white men offered trauma release sessions, followed by mandatory genital massages to show one's appreciation for the overcoming of their childhood wounds.

Bill and Hillary voluntarily threw in the towel and retired to Jeffrey Epstein's Orgy Island, were they finally had sex again, with the help of a team of tantra teachers flown in from Bali, along with extremely high doses of MDMA offered freely from Trump's new global company. They so loved their new life, they remarried, presided over by Marianne Williamson, and committed once and for all to the "monogamy of threesomes" – Bill, Hillary, and Bill's fantasy lover, as ONE.

Despite the comments by Hungary's commissioner Szilard Demeter, comparing George Soros to Adolph Hitler and wanting to turn Europe into a gas chamber, the multi-billionaire had enough ridicule and conspiratorial BS, so he returned to his native country, seized the presidency, took Joe's advice and surrounded the capital of Budapest with 10,000 armed guards who graciously agreed to share one portable toilet. He then demonstrated his unimpeachable virtue by giving all of his money to the people, except "that chunk of dark money" given to his fellow global elites to hide in Bitcoin, should he need it for a rainy day.

Bill Gates and other QAnon cult members, on the

other hand, opened a network of orphanages in Yemen and cultivated their blood fetish with traumatized children, and without fear of retribution. They were last seen giving each other vaccinations and telling each other, "I told you that we would find a cure."

Meanwhile, their cult followers joined them and together they started the Bill and Melinda Gates International Pedophilia-Rescue Commune for Homeless Children, of which there was no shortage, from the never-ending bombing by American-supplied Saudi forces, funded, no less, by Obama and Biden's $100 billion dollars in arms sales back in the day.

Both President Obama and the first lady Barrack chose to "live their best life" after coming out of the closet and committing to becoming transsexual, which allowed them to finally flesh out places in their marriage that had never previously been explored.

Word had it they retired on a secret island in French Polynesia donated to them by their friends at Big Pharma and the nuke industry, where they started a high-end nudist colony for elite neoliberal trans-couples.

On the other hand, the kids of America were not so lucky, and were told to work it out for themselves. As a result, they refused to home school any longer and started a nationwide ring of "unschooling" schools that sadly included Zoom drug parties and orgies. Thus, a new wave of influencers on Instagram Xtasy and Tik Tok Tantra Porn was born.

The good news, however, was that some of these fire-brand innovators became billionaires as young as ten. But were routinely picked up by Zuckerberg's underground splinter-group of San Quentin secret Zoom-police and put into penthouse cages to INCREASE their "Extreme-Greed-2021 Virus." This was done with the help of Silicon Valley's new pre-teen, ripped off version of OM's ETR-DMT assisted mindful-therapy-enhanced, to "BECOME AN INSANELY GREEDY MULTI-BILLIONAIRE by AGE 18."

Fortunately, the kids fought back and inserted a bug in the App called "Anti-Davos Malware," and escaped into the few forests that remained in California to live in nature and grow their own food.

Biden's hip hop heartthrob, Cardi B, finally rose to the peak of her success and became every young girls Gloria Steinem, and boys too, as her hit song WAP became both the new national anthem and theme song for TRUMP'S REVENGE – Save America and the World too Campaign, with the help of his company's NASDQ listed, "MDMA-assisted Global Psychotherapy Peace and Prosperity Program."

Thus was born the post Covid pre-extinction "Roaring Twenties II", and with it, to commemorate the greatest era in American history, a statue of Donald J. Trump was built adjacent to the Statue of Liberty in New York City. The only difference was that Mr. Trump's statue was 6 feet higher than the Statue of Liberty's 305 feet. It was the six feet of orange-cooper coating used for his hair that made the difference. As a final touch, an inscription was chiseled in stone on the base of the Statue that stated: "ME – the 47th in 2024."

MY DREAM TEAM

I hear the *Bodhisattva Maitreya*, our Buddha to be, talking through me from her celestial home in *Tusita* realm: "Alan, GET SERIOUS. The Clock's ticking. Societal collapse is upon you. The planet is poisoned from pole to pole. Extinction is underway. Stop dicking around with your cute political satire. And don't tell me it's from the acid or autism or Asperger's or your brain trauma. Enough excuses!

"Alan, listen up. You cannot do it alone. Think *kalayanamitta* – wise alliances. Call in YOUR DREAM TEAM and get down, together, in radical open dialogue. Only then will the TRUTH be revealed."

With humanity POISED at the crossroads, entranced with their supremacy, I called upon EVERY FORCE OF WISDOM in the cosmos to commune with me, to come through me. This is an SOS – an EXISTENTIAL EMERGENCY. I want to know my pantheon of *Dhamma* Warriors, my *Samsaric Sangha* – the finest minds that have influenced me throughout eternity. Please appear.

As the acid took me higher, I cranked Zeppelin's,

"Stairway To Heaven." As the music entered me, I heard Bob shouting through my veins, "Alan, this is the moment you've been waiting for your whole life. Ask the most challenging questions. Find the the most invigorating answers. Dive deep into your soul for meaning. Engage these wise voices, with heart. The future of FREEDOM IS IN YOUR HANDS."

"Alan, Hermione Granger here, your celestial sister from Harry Potter. I'm here to help you, Brother, in every way. I'll give you all of my sorcery skills to lend aid to your crusade to end the human onslaught on nature and save the world from its own ignorance. I am here for you, fully.

"But remember, Alan, there are no technological silver bullets to stop mass extinction, so do not be distracted by those who propose such nonsense! And most of all, as I said in the "Philosopher's Stone", bring those Savants to you who embody bravery, compassion, vision and most of all honesty. If you want to address extinction head on, you must find a different way of life. Rise up and FIGHT ON, Brother.

"And also, be careful, Alan! The post-Constitutional neoliberal forces of totalitarian communism will want to destroy you for addressing these issues and speaking truth to power. They will mock you and ridicule you and try to shame and cancel you in every way possible. Just as they have done to Chelsea Elizabeth Manning, Julian Assange, Edward Snowden, Robert Kennedy Jr. Greta

Thunberg, Extinction Rebellion, and of course, Donald J. Trump and the entire America First Movement.

"Those from the DEEP STATE are sociopathic. STAY STRONG. I am your sorceress on call, anytime. And keep the words of the *Buddha* alive in your heart: 'Hatred never ceases by hatred; But by love alone is hatred healed. This is an ancient and eternal law.'"

"Alan, Mohammad Ali here. Remember, it ain't over 'til the LAST PUNCH you throw. You must find an answer to the planetary emergency and end human supremacy and their delusions of green fixes to stop the planet's 1.5 billion cars that are used EVERYDAY to kill EVERYBODY to buy food so not to die. The MADNESS MUST STOP."

Then I hear the children of tomorrow in my heart, "And don't think that fossil fuel run nuclear power plants are the answer or that nuclear plants with carbon-capture systems will resolve the problem. Or that decommissioning every nuclear power plant will save the world when you can't agree of whether to wear a mask or not.

"Or that trying to remove all the plastics in all the oceans that will soon outweigh all the fish. Or building twenty story dikes to keep back the 130 feet of sea level rise ALREADY baked in from ice melts, in order to prevent fourteen of the world's largest metropolises from becoming aquariums, including New York, Shanghai, and London.

"Or blow hundreds of square miles of wind and

solar farms in our face like the farce that it is, consuming MUCH MORE fuel than the coal and carbon killing us NOW. Or better yet, outfitting the hundreds of millions of cows worldwide with methane capturing masks. WAKE UP GUYS. We want to be born and live in a safe and sustainable world. Figure it out, NOW."

"Alan, Sister Greta here again: You fuckwits. How many times do I have to tell you that you've stolen my dreams with your psychopathic fantasies. Goddammit, we're dying. Ecosystems are dying. Species are dying a thousand times faster because of us humans. We've had nearly two decades straight of the hottest years on record. GET IT, we're in the midst of a mass extinction event, and all you wankers can talk about is your obsession with consumerism, and money and deranged tales of American politics and NEVER-ENDING economic growth.

"And despite what you think, I'm not in the pocket of the Green New Thieves and Davos. In fact, your "Bright Green Lies," as Derrick Jensen brilliantly outlined in his book, are a coward's way of increasing the pace of human generated extinction.

"Screw all of you! Yes, I have autism, just as Alan does, and we couldn't give a shit what you think of us. So piss off."

"But we can save the future, Greta," the Eco-Elites shout back. "For $27 trillion dollars we can overhaul the entire energy sector and have a solar powered world in ten years. The entire world will be run by our sun."

"Listen up, knucklehead. I'm Greta Thunberg. Do you take me for a fool? You narcissists are too obsessed with your military toys to give up nuclear. Not to mention your extinction obsession through factory farming, clear-cut logging, mountain top removal mining, bottom trawl fishing, and need I remind you, your wholesale slaughter of nature. The predicament life is in, is not about lives, but LIFE ITSELF."

"Alan, Mai here. Let go. Civilization is killing itself. IT CAN'T BE STOPPED. It sold itself to machines and gadgets long ago. It's past the point of no return. Furthermore, it's all *pappanca*, mental masturbation. There is no world to save, Alan. Existence, as you know, yet keep denying, is a house of hallucinations burning with fear and ignorance. No lifestyle shift is possible at this point to prevent a catastrophic future.

"Release yourself from the delusion of safety in form. There are no winners with mass extinction. Step out of the house altogether, Alan. Seek your own release from the causes of S.H.I.T. Nobody can stop the Doomsday Clock at this point. Only by oneself can one stop their own clock.

"Hear me, Alan. Take the left road and walk into *Nibbana* – the Unconditioned. The Deathless. And leave the right road alone, as it leads to the world of Form, to Collapse, to Death, to Extinction, AND to an endless rebirth and redeath within *Samsara*."

"Alan, Jem Bendell here, author of the super-smart, ground-breaking paper, "Really Deep Adaption," that went viral, as you know. Frankly, I didn't go nearly deep enough with "Really Deep Adaptation." Truth is, collapse is happening NOW. When I say societal breakdown, I mean mass disruption, mass starvation, mass destruction, and global war. And I mean in your own life, Alan.

"Hear me, Brother. This is not like watching some animated Netflix series on "Extinction Part 1-6" from your villa in Bali. With the power down, you'll not have water for the pool or hot tub. You'll depend on your neighbors for food and, in our case, wine, women, and mushrooms too. You'll become malnourished. You'll become disoriented. You won't know whether to wear a mask or not wear one, or to stay in Ubud or move to Canguu.

"Moreover, you'll fear being tormented by marauding authenticity coaches as payback for this book, before forcing you to break your vow of sacred celibacy and finally have sacred sex. Before forcing you to do it again and again and again, until you finally fall in love. Pretty much the same way I'm adapting to extinction. By the way, lets catch up at Zest for a wine soon after the collapse. I'm fairly certain Bali will be spared."

"Alan, Jesus here. Only evildoers like the darkness of the right road. Take my Bi-Sister Mai's advice and I add my own, and please recite after me: "The LORD is my shepherd; I shall not associate with criminal Joe's selling out of America and his neoliberal corporate fascism today and global totalitarianism tomorrow.

"He and his "Big Brother" regime will force you to lie down in their climate-stricken barren consciousness and charred forest ruins: he will leadeth you beside the acidified dead ocean waters strewn with millions of extra mail-in ballots, Covid masks, recycled plastics, and too many miles of dead fish.

"Yet, I can restoreth your soul to walk out of the valley of Democratic self-delusions and leadeth you in the path of Republican righteousness over greed, profit and eternal white privilege.

"Yea, though I walk through the valley of the dark shadow of imminent mass starvation, new pandemics and a Davos-generated near-term extinction, I will fear no evil: for thou art with me LORD; thy rod and thy staff they comfort me.

"Thou preparest a table before me in the presence of my totalitarian globalist enemies: Thou anointeth my head with the courage to share the higher teachings of "OM assisted ETR-DMT mindful transformational shock therapy" freely, for all non-believers to return to a love of nature, mutuality and non-consumerism.

"Surely goodness and mercy and abundance shall follow me all the days of my life: and I will dwell in the house of the Anti-Totalitarian Trans-LORD forever." AMEN.

A CALL FROM THE PRESIDENT

I'm broken from my communion with GOD and my TEAM by an Emergency Warning Alert on my iPhone. I look down to read, "The 46th President of the United States of America, Joseph R. Biden, would like to speak with you – PLEASE PICK UP."

Instantly, I put the President on speaker and the House of Rocky fills with his dynamic presence. "Alan, Joe, here from the Oval Office. Let me be straight to the point, and not meander, as I'm so often accused. As a long-time operative for the Agency you're aware of your special Q code clearance. I wanted to call to both thank you for your decades of service to America and also inform you that your services are no longer needed. I'm retiring you, effective NOW.

"I also want to thank you specifically for your many years of devoted work with Burma's democracy movement and with Aung San Suu Kyi. The military coup in Myanmar is tragic. Dictatorship is WRONG. That your friend has been deposed and detained is unacceptable. I promise you that I will do everything in my power to have her released and democracy restored.

"As you know, Barrack and I are very fond of her. Meeting her in Yangon was one of the highlights of his Presidency. The same with Hillary. And of course, I was blessed to have had breakfast with her here in Washington. She's one smart Lady and a bright shinning example of compassionate leadership, as well as embodying the power of mindfulness in politics. America has a lot to learn from her unique skills and equally, from the courageous freedom loving people of her great country.

"On a more personal note, I've read your reports over the years as well as your books, both as a Senator and Vice-President, and found them fascinating. Your study of totalitarianism and the machinations of propaganda and mind control, as well as the power of nonviolent resistance and the necessity of protecting freedom of speech, have helped me to become both a better man and leader.

I will make sure that your four volume set, "Burma's Voices of Freedom: An Ongoing Struggle for Democracy," becomes mandatory reading for all staffers, Pentagon and Agency officials, and members of the House and Senate, especially now, as I determine our next course of action to support Aung San Suu Kyi.

"Further, I particularly loved reading "A Future To Believe In: 108 Reflections on the Activism of Freedom." In fact, I have a copy with me here on my desk, with many pages marked that I often refer to for day-to-day guidance.

"On a closing note, the Agency has given me a printout of your conversations today with yourself, with Shakti-Ma and your psychiatrist. As you know, it's evident that you're having a challenging moment. It is also evident that you have misgivings about me. I want to assure you, Alan, that I will not betray America. I will not undermine our great democracy. I will do everything in my power to uphold universal human rights, especially freedom of expression. You do not have to fear being ERASED as we are doing with so many other folks.

"All I ask, is a signed copy of this book. And please, print exactly what I am saying to you NOW, verbatim. I want you to hold me accountable to keeping my word. I want America to hold me accountable. I also want Aung San Suu Kyi and the freedom loving people of Burma to hold me accountable.

"Thank you again for your decades of work at the Agency. You are a true American. And when you're next in Washington, please let us know and the Biden Family would like to host you and your partner here at the White House, whoever it may be at the time. Just joking. I know you are a conscious celibate that prefers sapio-spiritual-sexual encounters, more than 'Wam! Bam! Thank you, Ma'am!' like my son Hunter, the most intelligent person I know.

"Last but not least, Donald, as is customary, left me a "generous note" here in the Resolute Desk. I'd like to read it to you and also encourage you to include it in your book.

The Former President wrote, "Dear Joe. I stand

committed to working with you and your Administration on healing our Great Country and making it shine like never before. Let our shared love for Universal Human Rights and the Sanctity of Earth prevail over profit and privilege and do all that we can to prevent societal collapse and the sixth mass extinction. Donald J. Trump.

"PS: I know you know, Joe, that your people stole the election, but I am going to give it you, nonetheless. I have this new company, called "MDMA–MAGA", that I'm going to focus on and make it the centerpiece of my 2024 Presidential campaign to "Save America Again and the World," after four illegitimate years with you, Joe. Even if you TRY TO PURGE me from POLITICS, I'll never GIVE UP. All the best. DJK."

"Alan, that is precisely why we have revoked your Q clearance. You are TOO CLOSE to Trump and we think he will remain A THREAT TO OUR GREAT NATION. Thus, the 10,000 armed troops and razor wire fences around the White House and Capital.

"Otherwise, everything else I said, stands. Stay alive. Your voice is needed more than ever, and hope to see you soon. By the way. I loved "Rocky." As you know, Bob was a major donor to Barrack and I. And the Former President and Michelle said to thank you as well for your fine service to America. They too hope to get a signed copy of your book."

THREE KINDS OF S.H.I.T.

Mai, the Buddha-to-be, returns, saying, "CUT. INTERUPT. REEL IN YOUR AUTISM. GET HOLD OF YOURSELF, Alan. This is not a real life "Truman Show" on acid, as much as you'd like to believe. This is LIFE and DEATH, YOUR OWN and THE PLANET, too.

"Let me frank with you, Alan, and remind you of my most salient two truths: "All beings wish to be happy and to avoid societal collapse, suffering, and mass extinction. Even the Democrats. Even the Communists. Even the oligarchs on Wall Street and Silicon Valley. Everyone, unless you are a sociopath or sadist, or both.

"You, on the other hand," seek happiness in the wrong ways, and as much as I love you as a brother in the *Dhamma*, as a consequence of your fear and arrogance and general misguidedness, you experience a lot of obstacles.

"Although you did well in Sister Shakti-Ma's session, you must once and for all break your self-defeating patterns. Frankly, I was expecting more out of you today, especially with the acid I arranged for you. But there's still time. Listen up.

"There are three kinds of S.H.I.T. in life. The first S.H.I.T. is called S.H.I.T. S.H.I.T., or in Buddha-speak, *dukkha-dukkha*. This is felt as bodily anguish, identical to the suffering you felt in Virginia Beach when you crashed your car into that telephone pole and went through the windshield.

"What you didn't tell people is that because of your traumatic brain injury you live in DENIAL, amplified by brain network malfunction and chronic tinnitus, and with them, sleepless nights, panic attacks and depression. I bring this up not to expose your lack of transparency, but to personalize the symptoms of the second form of S.H.I.T., known as *viparinama-dukkha*. This is called mental anguish.

"Even today, your contemplation of mindful euthanasia is an expression of this second form of S.H.I.T. And it would behoove you to share that your desire to take your own life is nothing new. And let me remind you, it has very little to do with near-term extinction and almost everything do with your unwillingness to embrace your vulnerability and equally, your unmindfulness of the mental state of anguish.

"The third form of S.H.I.T. is *sankhara-dukkha*. This form of suffering is the anxiety associated with impermanence. In that, nothing lasts. Every thought, every breath, every state of mind, are as ephemeral as bubbles on a stream. As with every birth and death. Every element of the universe is in flux, Alan. Nothing stays the same. You know this, but I am asking you to LIVE IT.

"And before I hand it over to the other honorable members of our DREAM TEAM, let me share in brief the 'Second Truth or the Cause of S.H.I.T.'

"Out of ignorance one desires and craves and grasps,

just as an octopus clings to a rock. You may think it's natural to cling as an octopus does. But unless you stop clinging to the rock of your earthly abode – stuck in your consumerist-habits through willful avoidance – you will not seek safety and walk out into the sky of FREEDOM – *NIBBANA* itself. The unconditioned primordial release from S.H.I.T. Only then will the suffering cease."

AN EXISTENTIAL DIALOGUE

"Alan, Michio Kaku here. I've been teaching quantum physics for decades. I confirm Mia's truth on factual scientific grounds. Planets come and go as do entire galaxies. Our universe is an endless realm of nuclear holocausts. Although life has survived a myriad of cataclysms, no place is safe, Alan.

"Even the extinction cycle we're presently in here on Earth, from our human perspective it's a slow motion disaster, but from a geographical reference it's instantaneous.

"Therefore, cease clinging. You are far smarter than the octopus. They'll cling to things that will harm them, even kill them. So, listen to the wisdom of Mai. Give up all earthly clinging and seek safe passage through an internal worm hole into the UNCONDITIONED. Only there will we find new horizons and perhaps fresh realistic hopes, beyond the need for anything external to thrive internally."

"Alan, *Bhaishajya* here. I'm a metaphysical Tibetan master of transcendental remedies. We were close friends in a former life. What I'd like to suggest is to draw the light rays of projection and death back into your own heart. In so doing, there is no loss, other than fear itself.

"From there, embody the transparent primordial impartial awareness that contains all things, but does not keep them. Stay within your own body, Alan, as it is the only vessel for enlightenment. There – inside of your own Being – you will find boundless life. A life far beyond the right or wrong of human supremacy and the fear of extinction."

"Carl Jung here, Alan: I have often said, I am not what happened to me. I am what I choose to become. Release yourself from historic self-references and limiting fixations. Embody conscious choice and live freely within the imperfect wholeness of your own natural uniqueness.

"And from there, become a cognitive snowflake, fearlessly forming and reforming in the kaleidoscopic sky of our infinite nuministic home. And I may add, keeping spiritually intelligent choice alive is far better than killing it and yourself through denial and or morphine."

"Alan, Brother Rumi here. I can't in good faith stay in the background any longer. I say, go beyond good and evil. Duality is a loser's game. Go out beyond your ideas of wrongdoing and rightdoing, and there you will find a climate-damaged field, Alan, with a dried up pond and burnt trees. I'll meet you there.

"When the soul lies down, Brother, in that special grass, sadly parched from the hottest summer on record, ideas, language, even the phrase "human supremacy" doesn't make any sense. Frankly, life is too full of BS to waste time even talking about saving the world, much less who voted for whom.

"So, I say, the breeze at dawn, Alan, has her secrets to tell you, and be clear – one of them is that your house is on fire. And please, don't keep using Ambien to go back to sleep. Break the habit. Now is the time to WAKE UP and ask for the woman of your dreams to appear. Only then will you find wholeness."

J. Krishnamurti fires back, "That's mighty poetic my Muslim friend. But the truth is, MAN is the only animal that is to be dreaded, and it's the supremacy of that dreaded dumb ape that is the problem.

"It may sound harsh when I quote my favorite Latin saying, *"Si vis pacem, para bellum"*. But the ancients knew "If you want peace, prepare for war." So, I suggest that governments ditch the vaccine, especially Pfizer's, and set up Covid infection centers and pay people to voluntarily infect themselves. In so doing, we go to war with the virus and develop "herd immunity" as quickly as possible.

"Then, for the more advanced among us, we have psychologists at each Center to explain to "herd volunteers" the wisdom of cultivating their compassion for the future of life, by depopulating the planet and mindfully euthanizing themselves. Rid our beloved Earth of the most stupid MEN among us and give the planet a chance to regenerate herself with a more advanced mutation of the species.

"My way of saying, the situation is utterly hopeless, unless there's a great die-off of at least six billion humans. Rid the ranks of the most stupid MEN first. Start with predator Priests. Then the C.C.P. ISIS. The Taliban. Pedophiles. Politicians. Onward to Wall Street... Believe me, there are a lot of powerful men who would much prefer pussy Heaven to a pandemic scorched Earth."

"Carl back. J.K., I have always thought of you as more refined in your knowledge of human consciousness. Surely you realize that knowing your own darkness is the best method for dealing with the darkness of others. Step up your game, dude. And you of all people, being born in India, should know that a woman's sex organ should be referred to as a *yoni*."

"Hey Guys. Stefan Z here from Austria. I saw Hitler's rise to power, and NO ONE listened to me when I said STOP HIM. And here we are again on the cusp of a new one-party totalitarianism with Wall Street and Davos in bed with the C.C.P., and I AM CRYING OUT TO YOU, AWAKEN, doomed brothers and sisters, that thou may save thyself from the "Great Reset." AWAKEN from your heavy slumbers, heedless ones, lest you be slain in your sleep; AWAKEN, for the walls are crumbling, and will crush you; AWAKEN."

"Alan, Emile Durkheim here. What Brother Stefan failed to tell you is that he and his wife Lotte took their own lives to "escape the crumbling." And I tell you in all fairness, I fully understand your own urge to mindfully transition. As I said in my book "Suicide, A Study," one cannot long remain absorbed in contemplation of the sociopathy of politics and the horrors of societal collapse without being increasingly attracted to their darkness. In vain, one bestows value on them, even freedom and infinity; but this does not change their true nature. When one feels such "value" in non-existence, one's inclination can be completely satisfied only by completely ceasing to exist.

"I say this to you, Alan, because I want you to live. So let me remind you of St Augustine's great summoning: 'Hope has two beautiful daughters, their names are anger and courage.' Let your anger build, Alan, until it sets hope on fire."

THE REAL BUDDHA APPEARS

Mai, I come back to you. I have given the *Dhamma* the best years of my life. I risked my life and freedom. I suffered many diseases. And now the Covid has set me back years. All this, to devote my life to those sacred teachings. As you know, I practiced my ass off. And now, I'm ready to call off the future and end it tonight. Who shall I believe, really?

"If you want to process the past, okay, I'll go there," Mai responds. "You did not listen to me well enough. I've watched some of your recent Facebook live-streams and I must say they are somewhat disappointing. Your over passion, hubris and lack of scholarship easily mislead people. You even sound a bit like Trump at times.

"Regardless, my brother *Gautama Buddha* made it clear in his *Kalama Sutta* – the discourse on the "true teacher," that you're fond of misquoting. He did not say one should not trust teachers because they are poetic, funny, charismatic, and or followed by many on their social media streams. To the contrary, they have value and many of them are genuine guides, innovatively progressive based on the times you're in. After all, money and profit and privilege are important to a healthy well integrated human life, especially in a world in collapse.

"Furthermore, ghost writers, speech writers, and literary agents are not to be frowned upon, nor seen as symptoms of selling out. If you have access to your inner Donald Trump and can afford them, why not promote your brand? In many ways, in this hyper-competitive new age Covid-driven wellness market of today, those elements are necessities, if you hope to make it online, that is.

"Yes, rely on yourself and a volunteer or two when you can't pay an assistant, publicist and social media firm. But be clear, even posers, frauds and hypocrites have value, because once they see their own shallowness and redeem themselves, they show others the power of self-honesty and redemption.

"Most of all, so long as you practice mindfulness from morning until night, regularly low dose, purge at least once a month and undergo regular breath work, then and only then can you trust what comes through as authentic and reflective of embodied presence.

"Otherwise, if you still have self-doubt, go back to school and get that Ph.D. you've always wanted in psychedelic-assisted psychotherapy and earn a real living for once in your life.

"Further, having a professional career will inspire a real woman, Alan. And it's high time you found a life partner to make your life complete. Just make sure she's over 30 this time out and please, get over your fetish for young *yoni* once and for all.

"Overall, best for you to leave all this enlightenment and extinction business to true *Dhamma* teachers, and those green-scientists, former oil company executives, and far left politicians who know what they're talking about. Get on with your life, Alan. It's now or never."

Suddenly, I felt like I wanted to purge, Ayahuasca-like.

As my mindful intelligence kicked in, I knew I was listening to the evil *MARA* – the personification of hypocrisy, neoliberal sell-out and mindful global destruction.

I immediately dismissed (almost all of) it as

propaganda. Drank some water. Did a warrior pose and a few back bends. Smoked 25 micrograms of DMT. Swallowed 100 micrograms of ecstasy. Laid down in the *Shavasana* corpse pose and tried to consciously die.

"Alan, not quite yet. Stephen Hawking here. As you know, I'm a physicist with a fetish for sex, so we have at least one thing in common. Be clear. The world's population has been doubling every forty years. Along the lines of what Brother JK-Murti said, if MEN are not immediately removed from the planet by year 2600, not only will humans be standing shoulder to shoulder, but electricity consumption will also make the Earth glow red."

"Chill man," Jimi Hendrix blazed back, "You white collar neoliberal con artists, flashin' down Wall Street, flipping that plastic fuckin finger at Alan and me; you're just hoping that my Bitcoin will drop and die. But Alan and I know we're gonna wave our freakin' FREEDOM flag high. Excuse us, while we kiss the sky."

"Keep it simple, Alan. Nietzsche here. He who has a 'why' to live – so long as it is not to spread neoliberal inspired totalitarianism knowingly or unknowingly – can bear almost any 'how'. And remember, he who fights with these globalist monsters might take care least he thereby become an authoritarian monster. And if you gaze for long into the abyss, the abyss gazes also into you."

"Listen up Alan, Baba Ram Dass here. *Namaste*, Brother. Bear with me here for a moment as I am just finishing up washing *Gurugyi's* feet, while he contemplates God yet again, with yet another 1000 microgram dose of acid I unknowingly had with me when I died on Maui and took rebirth here in Oneness Heaven.

"I want to read a passage from the 3rd Zen Patriarch of China – pre-C.C.P. – something you published back in '74 when we first met in Boulder at Naropa. It may hold more value for you today, than before. And if you don't mind, I'm going to ad lib a bit to modernize it. Pretty much how I do everything.

"The TRUTH has nothing to do with time and space or human supremacy, the Insurrection Act, artificial nitrogen fertilizers, ultra-violence, the need to BREAK UP BIG TECH, the bio-weapon that the Wuhan-virus really is, magical thinking, totalitarianism, veganism, 1984, expansionism, the DEEP STATE, criminal Joe's collusion with China, Peter Navarro's "The Art of the Steal;" who, by the way, got his doctorate from Harvard just after I was thrown out; fairy tales of endless economic growth, technological silver bullets, QAnon, geoengineering, "Bright Green Lies" – a must read, by the way – Hunter's hard drive from hell (check it out; it's a shocker), China's genocide of the Tibetans and Muslims, or even mass extinction. Here – we're hanging in the ETERNAL NOW at the ETERNAL crossroads WHERE a single thought is ten thousand years, give or take a few years. In other words, eternal means time doesn't matter.

"With NO TIME, there is no here, no there—no crossroads, no me, no you, no Joe, no Donald. and no others – but everything is always right HERE before our eyes NOW, as in, BE HERE NOW.

"HERE, the NOW is infinitely large and infinitely small: no difference, for definitions like climate collapse, consensus reality, mass species annihilation, the denigration of language, doublespeak, the death of the Constitution, the end of FREE SPEECH, Trump running in 2024 and winning (*Maharaji* told me so, and don't let anyone try to tell you differently), and even the Earth's 7.8 billion imperiled *homo-sapiens* are irrelevant. Why? When you live in Oneness, there are no other numbers, other than ONE.

"So too with existence and non-existence. Don't waste time, Alan, in arguments attempting to grasp the ungraspable, especially petty things like election fraud or nuclear war or the Doomsday Clock, or even the future of life."

I took a moment to let RD's wisdom settle in and pondered his sagacity. After all, he was the one who turned me onto acid, the *Dharma* of being HERE NOW, and to the teachings of China's 3rd Zen Patriarch.

As I mindfully reflected, I embodied President Joe Biden at a press conference from the White House, announcing a breakthrough with the climate crisis, stating: "Former American Buddhist monk and former CIA Agent, Alan Clements, turned me onto an ancient text from China, that dates pre-communist, pre-totalitarianism, pre-slave-labor, and pre-genocide of Tibet. He recommends that we not waste time trying to grasp the ungraspable. I hereby introduce the *Tao* of fracking, the Zen of Apocalypse and the *Dharma* of denying Death. Despite rejoining the Paris Accord, these new spiritual approaches will help to relax the eco-grief and anxiety of our impending mass extinction."

"Byron "turn it around" Katie here, founder of "The Work." Alan, I fully agree with Brother Joe Biden. Take the blame off others and turn it around. Ask yourself, 'how have you created mass extinction, NOT how mass extinction is doing you.' And before you answer, are you really going to let the end of All Life take your happiness away? I say, call me a Nazi, but even if we all die, keep the bliss, Brother."

"Katie, I could not disagree more. R. D. Laing here. If you've read my work, you will know I was a drug-loving, meditating psychiatrist, with a specialty in normalizing mental illness. With all due respect to your misguided understanding of the human psyche, your so called "WORK" effectively destroys someone by violence masquerading as love.

"And before you judge me, I too have been a

propagandist. After all my years of introducing re-birthing to tens of thousands of people, I am of the conclusion that we are all murderers and prostitutes — no matter what culture, society, class, nation we belong to, no matter how normal, moral, or mature we take ourselves to be. We are all utterly estranged from our authenticity. And that means you too, Katie."

"Wow. You folks take yourselves so seriously. Anais Nin here. Let me read from my dairy before Henry and I rendezvous for an opium-awakened erotic getaway in *Tusita*. 'Reality doesn't impress me. I only believe in intoxication, in ecstasy, in existential eroticism, and when ordinary life shackles me, I escape, one way or another, to make love with everything. No more walls for me, baby. Done."

MAI RETURNS

"Mai, here again. Anais rocks. Otherwise grab hold of yourself, Alan. This is no time to be dicking around with low grade humor and a bunch of old guy psycho-babble and crazy quantum woo.

"All *Buddha's* have taught the wisdom of the four Noble Truths in order to free oneself from S.H.I.T. I agree with the 3rd Patriarch, there is NO EXTINCTION TO STOP. And if you stop it, there's another one and another one, until the heat of impermanence bursts your very own Earth bubble, like a water droplet on a hot skillet.

Extinction is inbuilt to the operating system.

"As I have said so many times today: all ideas are mere concepts, illusions. As empty as bubbles on a stream, and if you do not see that you cannot outrun reality, you're Doomsday Clock will always be ticking.

"You of all people, Alan, should have learned this during your time in the monastery. Grasping phantasms in the sky of the mind is like squeezing a balloon of stale air. At best, you end up with hollow rubber, or worse, a used condom filled with the worn-out semen of your wet dream of magical thinking.

"And out of your own idiocy, you go on inflating your own emptiness again and again with dead air, your dream cum. Even your most cherished ideas deflate with time, Alan. Life is as empty as a used condom.

"The same with the climate collapse. You blew and blew up the balloon with the carbon of industrial civilization, without realizing how dead it would make the atmosphere from the start. And now that the balloon is collapsing, you have to let go. Throw the fucking rubber away and be done with it.

"All that is left is to respect the timeless principles of *anicca* (impermanence), *anatta* (emptiness of self), and *dukkha* (suffering). S.H.IT. IS the nature of existence, full stop.

"Go there, Alan. Chant after me. Make it real. *Anicca vata sankhara. Upada vaya dhammino. Upakituva nirujihanti. Tesang vupasamo sukho.* All conditioned phenomena are impermanent. Their nature is to arise and pass away. To live in harmony with this truth brings the highest happiness.

"You cannot outrun the laws of nature, Alan. Everything that ever was or will be is changing, right now. You know that. Embody this truth. Every molecule of being, every neuron, every atom, every photon, are bubbles on a stream. Let go, dear man; allow totality to breath on its own and move with the ocean of impermanence. Enter the felt reality of your wisdom, Alan, not your thinking about truth."

"Alan, Boris Becker here, author of "Denial of Death." I agree with Mai. Your premise for hope is built on an elaborate defense mechanism that is in response to your anxiety. It's true for all beings in every dimension of existence. No one wants to die. Some use drugs and sex and meditation and politics to try to cope. But I can tell you there is no amount of mindfulness or drunkenness or faux-enlightenments to assuage the existential stress of coming to terms with death and moreover, mass extinction.

"All your petty symbols of heroism within your *Mandala*'s Wheel of Life are empty, as is your futile War with *Samsara*.

"And even you, Mai, with all due respect to your so-called incalculable lifetimes in pursuing your dream of *Buddhahood*, are merely the shadow-like symptoms of

'*Bodhisattva*-delusion-disorder' and an elaborate existential defense mechanism. Which is not uncommon with your cultural conditioning."

"You missed the point, Becker Boy," Mai shoots back. "You can't abuse the *Dhamma* with your banal theories of consciousness. There is suffering and a way beyond it. And it has nothing to do with your college-burdened wrong views. Frankly, even your renowned "immortality project" is psychobabble. Pure pablum and typical of someone with your lack of true *Dhamma* training.

"Let me continue, Alan, before I was so rudely interrupted. The same is true with *anatta*: emptiness of self and emptiness of intelligence, like Becker Boy.

"Chant after me, please. *Anatta vata sankhara. Uppāda vaya dhamminō. Uuppajjitvā nirujjhanti. Tesa vūpa samō sukhō.* All conditioned phenomena are empty, especially bankrupt philosophies that have nothing to do with real Dhamma.

"Now let me remind you, anatta means: No You, No Me. Only empty phenomena rolling on. The self is an illusion. There is no unchanging soul or consistent unchanging subject to the infinite changing kaleidoscope of life.

"I'll say it again, life – this *Samsara* – is a S.H.I.T. infested nightmare of interrelated conditions. And you humans are cognitive flesh-draped crap castles with two-way orifices, stuffed with organs, blood, piss, feces and tumors.

"That, I may add, you obsess over, sticking anything you can into those orifices and call it a life. But how ironic, you get sickened and ashamed at what comes out of them holes, except your own narcissistic dumb shit words.

"Enter *Nibbana*, Alan. Let go of the suffering and, as I said, let go of this hopeless quest to stop the Doomsday Clock and once and for all release yourself from your own self-generated S.H.IT.

"And in closing, Alan. I see on Wikipedia that of the four billion life forms which have existed on your planet, three billion, nine hundred and sixty million are now extinct. By way of saying, Alan, free yourself from the crap castle. Otherwise, you and your species are next on the block."

"Alan, Sigmund Freud here. As you may know, I addressed all this religious nomenclature in my book, "The Making of An Illusion." Along with the range of other mental challenges you have, you're also suffering from undiagnosed *anosognosia*. In simple terms, it is the lack of insight. But in a psychiatric sense, it is a symptom of severe mental illness. It is experienced as an impairment in one's ability to understand and perceive his or her own mental illness. It is the single largest reason why people who think they are enlightened or have bipolar disorder or even ordinary narcissism like Trump, and Joe too, and so many other charismatic figures, yourself included, do not seek treatment. Sad, but true."

"Michio Kaku here again. History has shown that even great minds like Freud suffered *anosognosia*, so take his words in stride, Alan. He's essentially pointing to the development of realistic mindful perspective. Therefore, remember, extinctions and apocalypses and dystopian landscapes and cosmological nuclear explosions hundreds of millions of light years in size are natural to the cosmos and occurring at this very moment NOW. Ram Dass did get the NOW part right, but was pathologically disassociated from context.

"Even our closest neighbors, the six billion Earth-like planets in our visible universe that may very well have forms of Life on them, some far more advanced than our own, they too will go extinct.

"Galaxies upon galaxies in every dimension of infinity undulate with *anosognosia*-laden sub-atomic particles programmed by a godless god, forming and dissolving, faster than a streak of lightning in the night sky.

"There are countless extinctions going on simultaneously at this very moment NOW. Let that in. Extinction, as Mai said, is the nature of the universe.

"Infinity, Alan, is that snowflake Carl mentioned, forming, melting and reforming. And you think you can find an answer to 'why' it forms and melts? Or true safety from the incessant melt?

"As Greta said, 'fairy tales' will not save you, Alan. Nor anybody else for that matter."

"Carl Sagan here again, Alan. I agree with the Mai and Michio. Extinction is the norm. And you humans are picnicking on the beach of your illusions with an Earth engulfing tsunami ready to crash down any second.

"Wait guys," shouts Elon Musk. "Why do you think I've been spending all my PayPal and Tesla money, and Bitcoin too, on Davos-X, mansions, my hot x-wife, and Grimes (I love her so), a half dozen or so kids, my move to Austin, and Space-XXX. Either we're going to become multi-planetary and soon, or we're toast. And just in case, my AI investments may very well save the day, especially the new OM generated 4-D neural patterning ERT-DMT existential therapy app that Alan and I co-own."

Kaku shouts back, "Space travel is useless, Muskie, unless we shed our digital skins and learn how to dis-embody consciousness from biology and laser port as pure-energy-beings faster than the speed of light.

"Be clear. To survive as a species, we must rapidly evolve from our *Type I* planetary civilization, to a *Type II* stellar civilization, to a *Type III* galactic civilization. Even so, no type of civilization escapes extinction, nor, as Mai said, the law of change."

"Sir Isaac Newton here. I agree with the distinguished gentleman, Mr. Kaku. Back in the day when I invented the prism, colleagues were clueless to the fact that light was made up of an infinite range of colors. When I put LSD in everyone's tea and said, 'Guys, get ready for a few quantum fluctuations' and refracted a rainbow through the prism on the wall in front of them, they gasped.

"Some thought I was God. Others thought I was a Guru. Still others thought I was the second coming of Christ. The women, bless their hearts, wanted to have my child. But I was gay, I told them.

"Same with Muskie and Michio. I say, go for it, chaps. Listen, if I could come up with the prism four hundred some years ago, you can either devise a *karma*-nullifying app or find a more hospitable home than Earth and eliminate fraudulent elections and those neoliberal globalists with their nihilistic death wish for all Life."

"Once we master the phenomenology of consciousness," Kaku affirms, "we can explore inner and outer worm holes and possibly find self-correcting universes with infinite dimensions of novel intelligences devoid of suffering and infused with a rapture radiant stillness, likened to the Buddha's unconditioned *Nibbana*. But sadly, we cannot even learn how to harness light for all our needs, and we are still too scared – stuck, as it were, as explorers in a mold."

Newton shoots back, "I say it again. Coming up with that prism was no easy task. And if you don't figure it out, you'll suffer a fossil fuel death and soon. As Rocky said, "sustained perseverance is everything.""

"Charles Darwin here. Let me say this. If you do not up your game, you'll be forced to start evolution all over again, and likely begin as a sexless creepy crawly single cell living in some pitch-black rock hole seven miles deep on a dead ocean floor layered with fifty feet of plastic masks."

"Do the math guys," Elon states. "Charles is saying that's a long ass time before we evolve again to understand the power of AI and OM and Bitcoin, and way too long for me to go without sex... I'll be right there honey."

"Yes," Hawken says. "No matter what comes down on Earth, even if everyone went vegan overnight and every man used a condom, the sun will engulf the planet in 200 million years or less. Read my lips: You've run out of options. You are in an existential emergency. Move to another planet ASAP or die of mass starvation.

"And, make no mistake, if the C.C.P. bio-virus and or the Extreme-Greed-2021 virus doesn't take you out, there will be no sunscreen to protect anyone from 2030 onward. And those left alive will look like brown taco chips."

"Hear me, old guys," Greta shouts out through her super-charged autism. "Blah, blah, blah. It's all bullshit. Have you not studied Kierkegaard? Listen up: you numb-skulls are 'tranquilizing yourselves with the trivial.' Get over it.

"I told you before and I'll say it again, I don't want any more of your techno-barbarism and wanker magical thinking, nor your quantum fairy tales of cosmic adventure. Get it guys. People are suffering right NOW. Have you not read "Be Here Now?" It means right NOW. And I am suffering, right here and NOW, as well. Okay? We need solutions right NOW, old guys."

"Listen up, psychos. I can't take anymore. My name is Jeepers Creepers. I'm standing in as the temporary Commissioner for Decomposed Plant Life on the Planet, after my colleague Old Growth was tragically clear cut from the earth, and is trying to heal.

"You must STOP treating the natural world as human property. A few facts: you humans are 100 percent nature, but live behind a Firewall of Denial, thinking you are somehow separate or different. Do you realize that it takes one hundred tons of plants for every gallon of gas you burn? That's clear cutting forty acres of my family every time you fill your tanks. Said in another way; you've consumed more gas in the last two-hundred-and-fifty years than all plants grown on Earth over the past thirteen thousand years. That amounts to the heating of the atmosphere at a rate of 400,000 Hiroshima-sized bombs exploding every twenty four hours, 365 days a year.

"I'm sorry to say this, but truth must prevail. Thankfully, your END AS A SPECIES IS VERY NEAR. And I, Jeepers Creepers, on behalf of the Joint Federation of Nature – All Plants, Trees, Oceans, Soil, Sand, Rock, Fire and Air on Earth – can't wait to live free of the Homosapien predator magical thinking virus-ad infinitum. Fuck you!

"And by the way, be clear who helped us. President Donald J. Trump. He is the one who signed the bill that made animal cruelty a federal felony, saying 'these heinous and sadistic acts of cruelty must STOP. AKA, stop killing us.'

"Alan, let me continue. You know this from your time living as a monk deep in the jungles of Sri Lanka. Allow me to refresh your memory. Remember when you came across a fellow monk who was meditating at the foot of a tree and had attained a high stage of *jhana* – a supra-mundane degree of mental absorption. Do you remember your shock when he came out of the state and the army ants had eaten most of his left foot and a poisonous snake was wrapped around his neck?

"Remember, he asked you to not try to remove or kill the snake nor remove the ants, in order to preserve your precepts of "not taking life or harming nature." Rather, he would take his own life through voluntary starvation and went back into *jhana*. Soon after, the snake bit and killed him and slithered off.

"When the head monk came, he said to leave his body where it was for the other animals to eat. Remember, it was at that point you became so filled with horror by the predicament of life, that you said, 'I want to become two with nature and be reborn as a *Deva*.' The question to ask is, how can you, as a human, live in harmony with non-humans and nature? Not escape nature altogether."

"You can't," yelled the Chair of the Federation of Animals and Wildlife. "You are too greedy and too stupid and too mean to respect us animals. George Orwell was one of the only *Homo Sapiens* that GOT IT. Us ANIMALS suggest you read "Animal Farm" and memorize Our Seven Commandments. 1. Whatever goes upon two legs is an ENEMY. 2. Whatever goes upon four legs, or has wings, is a FRIEND. 3. No animal shall wear clothes. 4. No animal shall sleep in a bed. 5. No animal shall drink alcohol. 6. No animal shall kill any other animal. 7. All animals are equal."

"Hey guys, Deep Adaptation Jem Bendell just texted and said you need an Emergency Intervention with a team member here at the Earth First Eco-Anxiety Hot Line. Listen up. I have 1000s of call-ins from folks wanting to commit suicide and others curled up on the floor in anguish over the industrial scale genocide of all life.

"In order to befriend your eco-despair and turn it around into positive action you must realize that nothing can be changed until it is faced. As Brother Kalle Lasn said, 'start by breaking your social media fetish. The shit preys on you, fucks with your headspace, distorts your sexuality, scrambles your thinking and prevents any chance of living a liberated, authentic life. Every time you look at your fucking phone, yet another faceless algorithm plants a monetizing virus in your head to reinforce yet another nature destroying consumerist behavior. WAKE UP. STOP the ADDICTION.'"

Harriet Tubman pipes up. "When you want freedom more than anything, you will risk everything to break the chains. Trust me.

"Against all odds, when my Black bruthas and sistas broke from the white man's gulags in the South and came with me to freedom in Canada, I carried an AK-47. Someone get scared along the way and wanna turn back, they jeopardize all of us.

"I said, whoa, whoa, and put that muthafuckin' rifle tight to his forehead. And said, 'you keep going Brutha or ya fuckin' dead.' Although his two big white eyes bulged out like twin full moons in the night, he high-fived me and said 'Sista, you rock.'

"The LESSON: Sometimes you need an incentive to keep pushin' forward. Just like Rocky told you earlier. See you white folks, all freaked about your privilege. You scared of the bogie man of the climate breakdown that you fuckwits created with your fat cat supremacist's lifestyles. I say fuck you, whities.

"Now, if I was a vengeful type, I'd say death to you all. But as a freedom fighta upholding universal human rights, I tell ya: see this extinction thing as a shot gun to the head of all 8 billion of you Bitches. Now what will you do?

"And let me remind you, before I run off – that Biden

dude is not right. He ain't gonna make it any better. He's a sell-out to Green Lies and that totalitarian dictatorship over there in China and they got one crazy system of slavery. That makes Biden complicit with slavery. Now that he's in the White House, if he is to be trusted, he should show his good will by painting it black. Zebra is not good enough."

"Even so. Joe passed laws when he was working for Brother Obama to imprison our Black brothers and sisters. The prison population went up by tens of thousands. I wasn't down with that.

"I don't have the answer to your doomsday problem, but I say get rid of that Biden fellow by any means possible. Trump is a narcissist but he's no killer. Biden is a phony, wanting to supplicate America to the Oligarchs on Wall Street and to that evil slave nation of China. And for us Blacks, phony is evil. Plus, he's illegitimate. Get rid of 'em in 2024 or sooner. And before I go back to Canada, I want you to know I stand with Jon."

"Thank you, Harriet. Jon 'Midnight Cowboy' Voight here, just before the Doomsday Clock strikes 12. Let me say it straight: This is our greatest fight since the Civil War. It's the battle of righteousness versus Satan – yes, Satan – because those neoliberal totalitarian leftists run by the Biden criminal family, Wall Street, the fascist white media, and the six Tech Titans – Google, Apple,

Microsoft, Amazon, Facebook and Pornhub – are PURE EVIL. Take 'em out, any way you can. Or they will take us out, and soon. And get rid of Twitter too."

IT'S A BAD DESIGN

Here in the House of Rocky with Harriet's gun at my head, I'm communing with my dream team of freedom fighters, calling on the collective imagination to fight the monstrosities of militarism, electrification and the murder of nature, all life itself.

With the cold barrel of human generated extinction pressed firmly to my brain, my War with *Samsara* took on A NEW URGENCY. "Either you walk to freedom," Harriet demanded, "or you die here in cowardly gloom."

"Rise up, Alan," Bob reminded me. "Midnight is coming soon. Hit Armageddon with all you've got. Give EVIL a knockout punch."

I felt Socrates burning with King's "sacred rage," and I SCREAMED out at the Supremacists: "Fuck your hemlock. Fuck your thought control. I'll call upon any force and deity and use any language I want in the cathedral of my own conscience.

"I'd rather burn in full public view with my tongue cut out than be a passive martyr in your sick totalitarian play. As Brother Orwell said, 'For every record destroyed or falsified, for every book rewritten, for every picture repainted, for every statue and street building you rename, and for every date you alter', I refuse to be your faceless puppet and will commit every thought crime possible to confront your inhuman attempt to control the collective mind. My freedom is not yours to take and my death will be my choice.

"And fuck you, God; force feeding us your sociopathic world. With your theologians telling us to pray. Have more faith. Go deeper in meditation. Be more mindful. Consult the stars and cards and shamans and therapists for guidance along the way. All for what? To be raped, manipulated and murdered and made food for maggots and worms?

"You tell us to change our socially-conditioned brainwashed way of life; to slow down, become more aware and decolonize our consciousness. You mock us for our expansionism and our domination of nature. What did you expect? You give us a small green finite sphere spinning in an inhospitable darkness, and on it, force us to co-habitat with wars, viruses, bugs, reptiles and primates that kill.

"And then you treat us humans like slaves, co-dependent on programmed impulses to sleep and eat and shit and fornicate and kill and hate and rape. Every breath requires you.

"Look at the history of civilization that you puppet; endless wars and massacres along with your cruel mockery of our biological limits. The land is saturated with the blood of your madness. And you tell us to figure it out. That it's our *karma*. Our ignorance. Our inheritance. Our social dilemma.

"How dare you speak in tongues about our short-comings and your sordid fairy tale of oneness and endless evolutionary growth. You scripted an Earth careening at high speed into the wall of your Apocalypse. Yet you keep gaslighting us with your 'DIVINE CREATION' – which is more like a dark theater of horror than a sacred garden of honor and delight. And you just keep telling us to work it out, or die again, and again, and again in your perverse world of heaven and hell. Until we cease our programmed proclivity for domination, stupidity, religion, and war.

"What do you expect us to do? Become radicalists? Burn bridges? Blow up dams? Assassinate sick leaders? Swim with the whales and dance with the bears? Break sacred images on the altar of your perversity? Sabotage the electricity grid? Refuse to work? Create one huge off grid international community? Lace the reservoirs with acid and hope? Call for global acts of civil disobedience to stop extinction? Immolate ourselves in the halls of power to defy your death wish for us ALL? Why such a psychotic context? Well, guess what? You're wrong. It's a BAD DESIGN. It's a psychotic cosmos and you know it."

As Brother Malcolm X said, and I agree: "We must act in self-defense." God, you're a Sadist – a Hitler with a fetish for death cults. As Winston Churchill declared, "You were given the choice between war and dishonor. You chose dishonor and you will have war."

SCREAM

"The war is on, the fight has begun: I refuse to participate in your universe of aberrant atoms. Your laws are lawless. No good world would conceive of fascism and slavery and genocide and extinctions. I'd rather take my life tonight with dignity, than to weep for the dystopian years on the horizon of your hell."

I dropped to my knees in Bob's House of Rocky and summoned a final call to the great goddess of compassion buried deep within my heart. Through the tears I asked her, "Please give me the strength, dear Lady, to remove the diabolical DNA of domination animating through me and throughout this tortuous Wheel of Life. I want a world without war and hunger and fear, but it feels like an impossible dream.

"So with you, my love, as my soul witness, I must take my life tonight, just as Socrates did, and die in dignity. The fight with *Samsara* is a bleeding illusion. It's over. I have given my shadow my best shot. The victory is in conscience, not form."

I walked to the bow of my inner-Being and there upon our earthly Titanic, I sat cross-legged for a final moment before self-immolation into peace. And here I offer you,

LIFE, a final prayer – a hymn, a SCREAM, before empty-
ing the syringe into my arm.

Here is my acoustic suicide note shared with the emptiness of a BAD DREAM.

Life Has Died Today, Goodbye—A Dystopian War Cry for Futures Unknown

I had no reason to believe the lies...
Life died today and so have I ...
Not in form alone
But in everything
As in, no trace
No legacy
No memory
No spirit
Not even that
Not even zero
Nothing

And

We once Lived
fought
Killed
loved
Fucked
Denied
Warred

Ate ourselves with ruthless death love
And so what
Life lived
And Killed itself
Until all memory was
Engulfed by heat death

And now
Nothing
Not a whisper
A murmur
A memory
Nothing

Not you or me or History
Not even silence
Nothing

Such was Life
We knew all along
But refused to agree
On the rights of Living
and Fighting
And loving
And fucking

Nothing
But Nature
Life taking Life

No blame
Nothing

A big fucking
Astrophysical Vacancy
Of nothingness thunder

Not even a murmur
Of life once Lived
Nothing
Not even that
Not even
That
Other than you and your beliefs

I tied the band around my upper arm until a vein appeared. As final act of mindful presence I slowly lowered the needle closer to my arm and just as I was about to enter the skin I paused. And felt, and listened, and teared... Until a calm strong voice intervened, saying: "No, Alan. Don't. This is Franceska. Ava. Mai. Let's have a heart to heart. There is a better way to go out than this.

"Defy fear and sing, Alan. Hear the music in your soul before you take your life. Feel it as a pure vibration and sing out to the heavens, calling out to our fellow inhabitants spread across infinite galaxies and in every dimension of existence. Sing out: "Hey Jude, She has found you, now go and get her. Remember to let her into your heart.

Then you can start to make it better."

"I'm here with you, Alan. Let me into your heart. Let love fill your entire being and TRUST; trust in our love and the existential rebel in you that REFUSES TO GIVE UP, even NOW, standing on the bow of our earthly Titanic.

"You ask, is there one true action in the face of death? Is there a single enlightened deed to be done to either escape or to prevent societal collapse and mass extinction? Look what I did before I was taken out in a blaze of Nazi fury. I ask, what will you do? Go inside and feel and feel us too.

"Drop into the multiplicity of intelligences animating through us at this very moment NOW. Occupy as many of them as you can, Alan. Feel these *Dhammas* illuminating everything known and unknown, everywhere seen and unseen, large and small. And feel our love too, as boundless.

"Feel into these vibrating fields of energy, Alan. Nature. *Samsara*. LIFE. And me and you and us right now, in union together within the Divine Feminine, in all of us. TRUST, Alan. Franceska is your guiding metaphor for your return to LOVE. I am your archetypal lover. I am *Avalokiteshvara*, the next Buddha-to-be, and the first as a bisexual woman. And you, Alan, as my primary man.

"Now, be the Mother. Honor her. Every being enters the world through the woman's womb. Be the lover. Be the GODDESS. The giver. In breath. Out breath. Oxygenate this LOVE, Alan, with your mindful intelligence. Trust in the rightness of the Divine Feminine. Trust in the *Dhamma* laws and principles that govern this timeless tapestry of interrelated mystery. Trust in LOVE. Commit yourself, Alan, to UNCONDITIONAL LOVE and engage life with small daily acts of resistance, regardless of time, context, circumstances and attachment to outcomes. LIFE IS TO BE LIVED. LIFE IS HOPE MADE REAL. LIFE IS LOVE.

"Dedicate yourself, again and yet again, to this LOVE, and move forward with the courage to do everything in your power to remove from the genome of your own mind and being, from the very cosmos itself, EVERY proclivity to harm, denigrate and or violate, oneself or another, or IT.

"Commit yourself, Alan, with me, to a life of EXISTENTIAL REBELLION until we both REACH the DEATHLESS – the timeless unconditioned *NIBBANA* – the one and only true EXTINCTION – that of GREED, FEAR and DELUSION."

With an upsurge of energy revitalizing my courage, I heard the voice of my sacred *Dhamma* teacher, Sayadaw U Pandita: "Alan, how should you face extinction, you ask? The same way you have meditated for decades. Remember those two books you read that brought you to Burma at that pivotal crossroads in your life nearly fifty years ago? Ram Dass' "Be Here Now" and Mahasi

Sayadaw's "Practical Instructions on *Satipatthana* Meditation," the how to 'be here now and develop insight along the way.'

"Be present with what is, right here and now. There, you cultivate *Vipassana* – insight into the true nature of all conditioned phenomena. *Anicca*, impermanence. *Anatta*, emptiness. *Dukkha*, well, you know enough about the Truth of S.H.I.T., so we don't need to bother with it. Just be mindful not to blame others for the way you feel. Transform the S.H.I.T., in other words, into reconciliation, into the freedom beyond us and them. Beyond Republican and Democrat. Beyond all DIVISIONS.

"Also, be kind. Be loving. Be generous. Give back. Be forgiving. Be self-honest. And most of all, remember the essence of freedom in your day-to-day life: 'neither wish to live nor fear dying.' From that place of non-grasping, while always inspecting your authenticity for cracks, ACT on behalf of the greater good. And as your dear friend Bob has told you so frequently, "Never Give Up."

"That"s right, Alan. I'll tell you a final time myself. I love you and NEVER GIVE UP."

NEVER GIVE UP

"Alan, Buckminster Fuller here. You'll remember you were with me as I lay in state as a dead man in Cambridge Massachusetts back in 1983, very near to your place of Birth. Remember what I said before I passed on?

"People often say to me, I wonder what it would be like to be on a spaceship. And I always respond in the same way, Alan: you don't really realize what you are asking, because everybody is an astronaut. We all live aboard a beautiful little spaceship called Earth. And if the success or failure of this planet and of human beings and all other species depended on how I am and what I do: How would I be? What would I do?

"And I invite you today, Alan, to bring these two questions with you when you wake each morning. Along with a third question: When will you do it?"

"Alan, it's Mom. I've been with you all day today. I'm with Dad and Sayadaw U Pandita and Bob and Ava-Franceska-Mai, and everyone else you have every loved and learned from in your countless lifetimes in *Samsara*. We are here in Mai's *Sangha* in *Tusita* realm. You too will be here soon and you both will reunite. Before you arrive, you have some final earth-work and heart-work to do.

"Remember what I told you before I passed on: SLOWNESS IS EVERYTHING. Take the speed out of your life, Alan. Especially now with the pandemic and mass extinction on the horizon.

"Slow way, way down, son. There is no hurry to get somewhere in order to die. Remember the wheelchair I was in when you last visited me in the nursing home before I passed away. You'll remember, I could not even move the wheelchair because both of my hands were gnarled and painful with arthritis. Someone had to do everything for me. Feed me. Bathe me. Change my diaper. Get me out of bed and put me back in it.

"You are young compared to me at that time. You have so many good years in front of you and you are so healthy, compared to me. Go out into the light and look up, Alan. Run wild. Return to nature. Yes, life has its darkness. But keep lighting candles. It is only light that dispels the darkness.

"Use your life wisely, son. Live, love, and laugh. It will not last. And remember, slow it way, way down. Take your time when you eat and drink and make love again. And slow it way, way down. Be mindful. Use your intelligence. I love you. Love yourself.

"And Alan, all of your friends are here with you and WE SAY, KEEP SCREAMING at the atrocities UNTIL WE ALL turn back that fucking CLOCK and BRING DOWN totalitarianism, human supremacy, nuclear weapons, the human death machine of consumerism and mass extinction. WE WILL NEVER GIVE UP. We are with you."

"Alan, Fergus here, as you know, we've been unstoppable friends and colleagues for so many years now and how blessed I am to be seen by you, to co-author books together, and to serve you as your assistant for nearly two decades. I've been tuning in all day, waiting for this moment NOW to share my most soulful truth with you.

"We are alive, Alan, because we have a sense of

MEANING. We DO NOT GET IT from the BBC, CNN, Donald Trump, Boris Johnson, Joe Biden, the Archbishop of Canterbury, Q of QAnon, Orpah, Deepak, Freud, Terry Pratchett, Tolkien, Putin, Premier Xi or anyone else, so how could WE lose it through their bankruptcy? We get it from our *Dharma* practice. We get it because we feel the living, real world presence of the ongoing mystery. We know that by now we are almost unstoppable, and that we've had both the courage and fortune to pursue things we think mattered and made a difference, rather than earned us any safety, security or company. There is NO FORCE in this world that can take away OUR sense of meaning save a thorough and lengthy bout of brain shattering torture. YOU MUST STAY ALIVE, my friend, for OUR WORK together has only just begun."

"If I may, before we close the show, a word from Aldous Huxley here. Let me be straight, Alan. The Brown Shirts of the Fourth Reich are everywhere today. I said it back in the day and it never had more importance than now: It is perfectly possible for a person to be out of prison and yet not free — to be under no physical constraint and yet to be a psychological captive, compelled to think, feel and act as the representatives of the nation State want them to think, feel and act. In other words: If you do not keep liberating your freedom, your freedom will imprison you."

"Somewhere, something incredible is
waiting to be known..." Carl Sagan

I recommitted myself to LIFE today, and the
courage to face whatever, come what may,
and the courage to ACT for the greater good.

The LORD will fight for you; you need only to be still.
Exodus 14:14

"And Never Give Up."
Robert Chartoff

Lightning Source UK Ltd.
Milton Keynes UK
UKHW010932120522
402883UK00002B/53